ALSO BY SNOOK

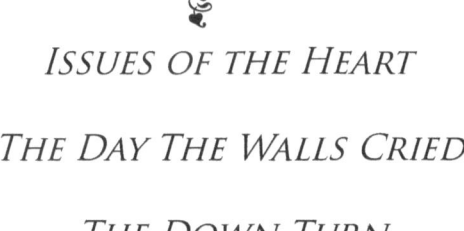

ISSUES OF THE HEART

THE DAY THE WALLS CRIED

THE DOWN TURN

KARMA'S KISS

A novel by
SNOOK

AMARQUIS PUBLICATIONS

 AMARQUIS PUBLICATIONS

Amarquis Publications, LLC
P.O. Box 34224
North Chesterfield, VA 23234

Copyright © 2011 by Snook

Library of Congress Control Number: 2015946175

ISBN: 978-0-692-48740-2

Second Amarquis Publications Paperback Edition July 2015

Printed in the United States

Cover art & interior design by IndieDesignz.com

ACKNOWLEDGEMENTS

The glory and honor belong to God for blessing me with the words to complete this novel. This book would not be possible without the support and encouragement from my family. I'd like to thank my children for understanding the long hours on my computer. Mommy loves you! Words can't express my gratitude to my family, friends, and everyone that supported me during this journey, thank you. Every encouraging word was greatly appreciated

To my readers, I hope you enjoy reading this as much as I enjoyed writing it. As this is the second edition of this book, I must say thank you to the first readers and supporters. We are back bigger and better than ever!

Much love,

Snook

This book is dedicated to anyone that has been kissed by karma. Good or bad, we all reap what we sow.

KARMA'S
KISS

CHAPTER 1

Suga

At the age of sixteen, I died. A piece of me was lost, and I struggled to find it. Her death was the end of my life as I knew it. I remember waking up to a blaring alarm clock on my pink nightstand. As I pulled the heavy comforter off of my head, it slipped off my scarf.

It was cold in the house since the pilot light was out. The clock read six o'clock in bright green digital numbers. I could smell bacon and coffee in the air, which meant my mom was in a good mood. Every Friday she cooked a big breakfast for me. On other mornings, I never got up on time to cook myself breakfast, so I settled for cold cereal or oatmeal.

"Suga, I know you hear that alarm clock going off! Come on down here so you can eat your breakfast!" my mom yelled through the cold house.

"I'm coming, mom!" I yelled back.

SNOOK

"Don't make me come up there, girl."

Although the house was cold, I'd sweated through the two pajama tops, two pairs of pajama bottoms, and two pairs of the thickest socks I could find. I hit the snooze button just in case I didn't make it out of the bed on the first alarm. I sat up on the edge of the bed as my wrap fell down to my shoulders. I slipped my feet into my two sizes too small, black furry slippers that sat on the floor beside my bed. Tired from my late night of watching television, I remembered my mom telling me to turn off the television. Instead, I turned down the volume and prayed she didn't come into my room to check on me. I could feel the heaviness of my eyelids from being so tired. Trying to appear rested, I walked downstairs for breakfast. Months ago, the table would have been set for three. My father, Linwood was arrested. He was missed. I knew he physically wasn't able to be with us, but I hoped that would soon change. In the past, he kept late hours and missed seeing me off to school most mornings.

I appreciated the times my mom cooked breakfast. We sat at the table together and enjoyed crisp turkey bacon, scrambled eggs, grits, and toast. She had even served fresh squeezed orange juice. After many attempts to make up for my father's absence, she eventually learned that she couldn't. I knew where he was and that he would be away for a long time. I put on a smile so that I didn't upset her.

"Your father is going to miss this party. That bastard," my mother said.

She blew white smoke into the air. Cigarettes were her new habit aside from shopping. In the past few months, our shopping sprees had become more expensive. I wondered where all of the extra money had come from, but I dared to ask.

"When is he coming home? I thought you said you were going to bail him out last week," I asked. I sipped my orange juice.

"I know what I told you. Things aren't that simple. Your father is being accused of some serious charges. Just know that I'm working on it." She pulled a drag from her cigarette.

"I know you are, but I miss him."

My mother told me that same story every week. I eventually realized that she wouldn't bail him out.

"I'm sure he misses you too, Suga. He will be home soon enough."

"When he calls tell him that I love him." I looked down at the scattered eggs on my plate.

"Baby, why do you look so tired? You weren't up all night watching those shows again were you?"

"No. I wasn't looking at the television all night. I don't feel good. Can I stay at home today?"

"No. You're going to have perfect attendance, my lady. You're not missing school for a stomach ache," she said, putting her hand on her hip.

I knew she wouldn't go for it, but it didn't hurt to try.

"Mom, please. I don't ask to stay home often." I put my hand on my forehead like an over dramatic actress. "I don't feel well."

"You can stay at home this time. Since you're too sick to go to school make sure you stay in the bed today," she ordered.

SNOOK

She placed the dishes in the sink. "No phone calls and don't go outside. You understand me?" she demanded while pointing her finger.

My back was towards her as I rolled my eyes. She always laid down rules to stay home, clean up, and no phone calls. Any other day, school would've been a better option. Going along with the painful rules she laid out, I agreed to stay home and catch up on my rest. There was something distracting that kept my mother withdrawn. It was obvious she had something on her mind. I knew she planned a party for that Saturday night, and she had a lot of work to do. Shopping bags covered the dining room and living room floor. When my mom planned a party, she always went all out. From the decorations, to the food, to the fancy party favors, she settled for nothing less than the best. I wasn't allowed downstairs during her parties, so I never offered to help. After picking over my food, I went to my room and snuggled back into bed.

I woke up around three o'clock that afternoon. The house was noticeably quiet. My mother was either resting or out running errands. Waking up with a dry throat, I headed to the kitchen for a glass of water. As I dragged my feet across the hardwood floors, I waited for my mother to scream out, *Pick up your feet, girl!* I had a habit of making scratching sounds with my slippers. There was nothing but silence.

Before reaching the bottom of the stairs, I noticed the front door was open. I looked around nervously as I slowly walked down the stairs. I tiptoed to the front door, peeked out, and found no one. There was an overwhelming presence in the house that felt as though someone was standing behind me. With fear overtaking my body, I quickly turned around to see if someone was there. As the air ripped out of me, I looked down, and that was when I saw her.

I felt light-headed due to the lack of oxygen from the blood that rushed from my brain. I grabbed onto the staircase banister as I tried to find the air to breath. With my feet glued to the floor, I dropped where I stood. The seconds seemed like hours as I collapsed to the floor in shock. My mind screamed, *go to her*, but my legs wouldn't move. I grabbed my stomach as sickness brewed inside of me. The sight of her made the sickness creep up to my throat. When I could finally get my composure, I screamed to the top of my lungs.

"No! No! Mom! Somebody help me! Please help me!"

I watched as my mother's lifeless body lay on the floor. The chair behind her was the place where she took her last breath. Time stood still. The sound of the grandfather clock on any other day would have gone unnoticed, but that day it ticked loudly with each second that passed. I crawled slowly to her on my hands and knees. My hands slowly covered my mouth. Trying to contain the screams that fought their way through my fingers, I reached for her body in agony. I struggled as I lifted her head and placed it in my lap. I carefully looked at her eyes that stared back at me. Her long dark hair covered her round almond colored face. As I gently moved her hair out of her face, I noticed blood and a powdery residue around her nose and mouth. My tears dripped onto her face as I looked at the saliva that hung from her mouth. I leaned down to see if air escaped from her nose and mouth and there was none. I placed her head on my chest as tears poured down my face in agony. Her chest was still with no rise and fall. I held her tightly and unleashed a cry that I pray will never enter me again. The pain that hovered over us had consumed me. I now realized that my mother was dead and gone forever.

Looking through my tears, I saw a cloudy silhouette. As I wiped my eyes, I looked up and realized it was my neighbor, Mrs. Lowell. She stood in the doorway with widened eyes. Holding her chest as if she had a heart attack, her reaction was the same as what I'd felt. Mrs. Lowell rushed through the door and searched for the phone to call for help.

I felt lost and alone. I hoped someone would wave a magic wand over her so things would be as they were that morning. As I continued to cry, I prayed to God.

"Please don't take her from me. Wake her up. Lord, please, help me," I said, as she lay in my arms.

The neighbors gathered on the front lawn. They peeped in trying to see what went on inside. Quiet gasps lingered from the small crowd that formed outside. No one dared to enter the house other than Mrs. Lowell. Hatred for them built up on the inside. I needed someone to help us to heal my mother's wound and to breathe life into her. However, I knew all too well that only God had the power to do that.

"Help her, please! Don't just stand there!" I shouted to the nosey neighbors. "Help me!"

"What happened to Teesa?" a neighbor asked.

"I don't know," Mrs. Lowell said, as she stood over us.

The crowd quickly grew, and the whispers were easily heard.

Why doesn't someone help us? Why are they standing outside and just looking at us? Do they see me sitting here with my mother's head in my lap? Is this a dream? I thought.

Mrs. Lowell was the only one in my dream that appeared real. While speaking to the 9-1-1 dispatcher she leaned down to my mother's chest to listen for her heartbeat. She lifted her limp arm and checked for her pulse. Through the hollow sound that was in my head, I heard her relay the information to the dispatcher. She kneeled down beside me and prayed. Tears fell from her eyes. Mrs. Lowell had confirmed what I already knew.

"No!" I yelled out. "God, please don't take her from me! Please, get up! Please, don't leave me!"

I shook her violently, hoping it would wake her from her deep sleep. My gut told me what my heart wouldn't accept. She was dead.

I can't live without her. I don't want to live without her, I thought.

I wanted to die right there beside her. I wanted to lay down beside her, hold her hand, close my eyes, and follow my mother to what I always believed was a bright white light in the sky. I wanted the pain in my heart to go away.

There was no way to prepare oneself at the age of sixteen on how to deal with finding your mother's dead body. As we waited for the ambulance, I rocked my mother in my arms and continued soaking her in my tears. I fought back nausea and let the tears flow as they fell heavily onto her body.

SNOOK

Afraid and needing someone to save me from that nightmare, Mrs. Lowell remained by my side. She quietly sent up all the prayers she had as she rubbed my back. She placed the other hand on my mother while she spoke to her spiritual being. Her presence was comforting, but it didn't change what was happening.

Minutes later, the sound of sirens blared outside. A heavy knock on the already opened door startled us. Mrs. Lowell met the firefighters, police officers, and detectives at the door. I looked towards the sound of the voices that entered the house as heavy boots hit the floor. Mrs. Lowell's head hung low as she stood at the front door looking at us.

"Somebody hurt this poor girl," Mrs. Lowell said, pointing to us. "It's a blessing they didn't hurt that baby there," she sobbed.

The paramedics rushed over to offer aid to my mother. A suited detective approached us.

"Do you live here miss?" the officer asked Mrs. Lowell.

He pulled out his notepad and took notes.

"No. I live next door. I heard that baby and ran right over. I thought it was her mother and father over here fighting. In the past, I would hear them all the way to my house around this time of the day. They would be cussing, fighting, and carrying on," Mrs. Lowell stated. "I knew that couldn't have been right because her father is in jail."

The officer jotted in his notepad as much information as Mrs. Lowell offered. From watching my late night TV shows, I knew detectives loved it when potential witnesses talked and shared what they knew about crimes. If it weren't for the witnesses, most crimes would go unsolved. The detective listened as he allowed Mrs. Lowell to continue without interruption.

"Before you ask, I ain't seen or heard nothing. I would tell you if I did. Now get on over there and get that girl out of here. She doesn't need to see this. She can come over to my place if need be," she said sternly.

The detective nodded to the officer to assist me.

While the firefighters, paramedics, and police officers walked around the house, I sat in my mother's residue in complete shock. I didn't know where they were taking her.

Was I going to end up in foster care or one of those group homes I'd heard about at school? I thought.

I watched as the officers rumbled through my mother's belongings throughout the house.

Frustrated, I yelled, "You have no right to touch her things!"

"Honey, we're here to do our job and to help her," the female paramedic said.

I could see and hear her speaking, but the words floated aimlessly in my head. I couldn't respond.

"You can let her go now. We're here to help you," the paramedic stated.

I held on to my mother tightly as the paramedic tried to pull her from my arms. As I fought not to let her go, the paramedic nodded to the officers who were nearby.

"No, no, no!" I yelled while kicking and screaming. The officers tried to pull me away from my mother as I fought harder. For a moment, it seemed as if she was holding on to me. I tried to wipe some of the residue and blood from my mother's mouth and nose. I wanted to make sure that she wasn't breathing. The world as I knew it instantly fell apart before my eyes. There was emptiness in the pit of my stomach. As I slowly let her go, I took one last look at her as an officer picked me up off of the floor. I was slumped over as the officer carried me outside. I took a mental image of the faces of those that didn't help us. The shame written on their faces followed me to Mrs. Lowell's house.

"I know this is difficult, but you need to tell us who did this to your mother," the detective said. "Was there someone else here with you and your mother today? Why didn't you go to school? Any information that you can provide will help us with our investigation."

I was overwhelmed with all of the questions, the detective's voice played like the teacher on Charlie Brown. He wanted to get as much information as possible from me, but I didn't want to hear anything the detective had to say.

"I don't know! I don't know! Please help my mom! Oh God, please don't take her from me!" I cried.

My mother was gone, but I continued to pray. The detective realized that I was too upset to provide any information, so he left me alone. My mother was happy and had planned her birthday party. At that moment, she was to be carried away in a body bag marked for the morgue. It was too much for me to handle alone. It felt like an outer body experience, and I watched my life flash before my eyes.

With my father in jail and unable to do anything to help me, my life changed in a blink of an eye. I completely shut down. There were many thoughts that caused havoc in my mind.

Mrs. Lowell took me to a back bedroom that belonged to one of her sons. Two of her three sons had families of their own while one still lived at home. The room had a twin bed with army camouflage sheets. No one had slept in the bed for a while. The dust from the room smelled like mothballs just like the rest of her house. The old stereo played Mrs. Lowell's *O'Jay's* record.

"Lay here, honey," Mrs. Lowell said, dusting off the bed and fluffing the thick pillows.

"No, I don't want to sleep. I just want my mom," I cried.

I stood in the doorway watching Mrs. Lowell's feeble attempt to make the bed as inviting as possible. I didn't want to rest.

"Look, child, come on over here and rest yourself. You don't have to sleep, but you will rest yourself. I'm sorry about what has happened to Teesa. You will see that life will go on. You may not understand it now, but you will," Mrs. Lowell said with sadness in her voice.

"It hurts and I miss her already. I can't see myself living without her," I cried.

I lost it again, and let out cries that I didn't know I had. I ran over to Mrs. Lowell and buried my teary face into her chest.

"I know it hurts, honey. Just let it all out," Mrs. Lowell said while holding me tightly.

I felt safe in her arms. I could feel the love and compassion she was giving me. I didn't reject it. I allowed it to soothe my pain and quiet me down. There was no way she would leave me alone. I no longer trusted myself as thoughts of suicide skipped through my mind. I thought of ways to kill myself without inflicting pain.

Slitting my wrist would be too messy and painful. Taking a bottle of pills would get the job done if I could swallow all of them, I thought.

Anytime I needed to take pills my mother crushed them up, put it on a spoon, and dipped it in applesauce. The constant thoughts of her made me upset once again.

"Suga, why don't you try to rest yourself until your uncle comes for you," she said.

Mrs. Lowell tried to pry my arms from around her waist. I held on tighter as I squeezed her waist.

"No, don't leave me in here!"

"All right, then I'll sit with you."

She realized that she couldn't win the emotional fight.

I laid my head down on Mrs. Lowell's lap and continued to sob. She hummed a tune while running her fingers through my hair. Her presence was comforting. It still was not enough to take away the pain in my heart. My heart physically hurt, and I couldn't understand how that was possible. Holding on to Mrs. Lowell was the only way that I could breathe. If I let go, I believed that I would suffocate.

CHAPTER 2

Redd

M r. Johnson, this is Mrs. Lowell, Teesa's neighbor. I'm sorry, but I have some bad news."

I could hear Mrs. Lowell sigh loudly. I sat down on the couch while she continued.

"Something has happened to Teesa. I called the ambulance, and they're over there with her now. I'm sorry to have to call you with such bad news," she said as calmly as she could.

I sat up at attention and shook my head as if I were in a bad dream.

"Where is my niece?" I asked in a shaky voice.

"She is here with me and the detective. I told the detective it would be fine for her to stay here until someone came for her. I think you should get here soon. She needs you. The detective would like to speak with you," she said.

I'd given Mrs. Lowell my phone number when Teesa moved into the neighborhood. Being the oldest of three, I was the big brother to Teesa and her identical twin Sable. I made sure Mrs. Lowell could contact me in case of an emergency. Neither Sable nor I had children, so we both spoiled Suga.

"Mr. Johnson, this is Detective Shepherd with the Richmond Police Department. Is your sister Teesa Johnson?"

"Yes, she is. What happened to her?"

From the sound of things, it wasn't good.

"We received a 9-1-1 call from Teesa Johnson's residence placed by Mrs. Lowell. Upon arrival, we found Ms. Johnson deceased. Her daughter, Suga, was with her at the time, but was found unharmed. At this time, she is here with Mrs. Lowell where an officer will stay with her," Detective Shepherd explained.

I tried to find the words to ask the questions that I needed to be answered. Everything the detective said played in my head.

"I understand, but what happened to her? Do you know how she died?" I asked, feeling as though my questions were avoided.

"We're still investigating, but there were drugs found at the scene. At first glance, it appears to be an overdose." The radio blared into the phone. "We won't know conclusively until the medical examiner makes that determination. I'm so sorry for your family's loss Mr. Johnson," Detective Shepherd said regretfully.

"Drugs?"

"Mr. Johnson we will allow you to come for your niece. Is that possible?" Detective Shepherd asked.

"Yes. I'm on my way now," I said. I put on my shoes.

"In these cases we try to let the child be with a family member. Because your niece is a minor a social worker is on the way to the scene to get some information from you," he added.

After hanging up, I fell to the floor in agony. Tears ran down my face. In a million years never would I have thought I'd have to bury my baby sister. I couldn't believe what I heard. I couldn't grasp the fact that Teesa was dead. I had to pull it together and see what happened.

"Redd, what's wrong? Are you all right," my girlfriend, Alyssa, asked.

"Teesa—" I was breathing heavily and felt my world crashing down on top of me.

With a feeling of defeat, I sat on the floor for a few moments. "What happened to Teesa? Is she okay? Where's Suga?" Alyssa asked while panicked.

"I have to get over there and find out what happened," I said.

The sound of Suga's name gave me the strength to get up off of the floor.

"I'm coming with you. You aren't in any condition to drive," she said while grabbing her purse and following behind me.

An hour before, I came home from working a double shift. I was functioning on little sleep.

"No, I'll be fine. Just get the guest room ready for Suga. She may have to stay here with us," I said, as I looked at her with pain in my eyes.

I stood at the door, realizing that I was walking into a world that was changed. I lost my sister, and the world felt much colder.

SNOOK

"Are you sure you can drive?" she asked.

Alyssa stood behind me with her hand on my shoulder.

"Yes, just have the guest room ready for Suga, okay?"

I didn't want Alyssa to see me breakdown.

I jumped into my white Cadillac Deville and headed to I-95. I knew I had to step up and take care of Suga for Teesa. Teesa always told me that if anything happened to her that I was to make sure I took care of Suga. Honoring her wishes was my first priority. I loved Suga as my own. She was the reason I never rushed to have children of my own.

The street approaching the house was surrounded by a crowd of people. The street was blocked by police cars, fire trucks, and an ambulance. The crowd was controlled by police officers and barricades. There were bystanders crying and comforting one another. Most of them appeared to be watching a television show. I became angry as their faces gave speculation as I approached the house that was surrounded by yellow tape.

"Excuse me," I said. I navigated my way through the crowd.

"That's Teesa's brother, Redd. Oh shit, it's about to get real. He knows Linwood had something to do with this," a voice said in the crowd.

Hearing the comment loud and clear, I ignored it and kept walking. As I made my way through the crowd in search of a police officer, I spotted a young officer on the opposite side of the tape. I waved my hand to get the officer's attention.

"I'm looking for Detective Shepherd," I said.

"Sir, step back. This is a crime scene," the officer ordered.

"I need to pick up my niece, Suga. I spoke to Detective Shepherd, and he told me to come here to pick her up," I said in a frustrated tone.

I was pissed at the officer as he brushed me off while avoiding eye contact with me. The officer upset me a great deal.

"Step back, please! No one is allowed past this point," the officer continued to shout to the crowd.

"Who is in charge here?" I asked. "I was called down here for my sister and niece. I understand you have a job to do, but I need to pick up my niece. My sister just died! Do you hear me?" I walked closer to the yellow tape.

At that point, I would have crossed the yellow tape with or without the officer's permission. We stared each other down as the crowd grew quiet, anticipating who would make the next move. Just when I was ready to explode on the insensitive officer, I heard my name called. Instantly, I snapped out of my rage.

"Are you Mr. Johnson?" a detective asked.

He was standing nearby talking with his superiors.

"Yes, I'm here for my niece," I responded, giving the rude officer an evil look.

"Let him through. I'm Detective Shepherd," he said.

I was allowed to cross the tape and lead to Mrs. Lowell's home.

"Give me a minute," I said, as I leaned against the house.

It took a moment for me to pull myself together because I didn't want Suga to see me upset. I stood outside of the house and took deep breaths. I could only imagine what state Suga was in.

"Take all the time you need. I completely understand. Nothing can prepare you for something like this. I will assure you that we will get to the bottom of this," Detective Shepherd said empathetically.

"You better because if I find out that he did this—" I stopped myself and pounded my fist into my hand in anger.

"Hold on now. I beg you to let us handle this. If not for nobody else, do it for that little girl in there," he said. He pointed towards Mrs. Lowell's house. "She's going to need you. From what I'm told, your sister was a good mother," he added.

"You're damn right she was."

After speaking with the detective, I pulled it together, walked up to Mrs. Lowell's door, and rang the doorbell.

"Who's there?" Mrs. Lowell called out.

"It's Redd, Teesa's brother. I'm here to pick up Suga," I said calmly.

"Come on in. It's open," she replied.

Detective Shepherd and I entered the dark home. Mrs. Lowell and Suga must have been in the house using the daylight, and didn't notice that the sun had set. Detective Shepherd and I followed a humming sound to a dimmed bedroom where the two of them sat on the bed.

Suga's head lay in Mrs. Lowell's lap as I watched her stroke her hair. Suga's arms were wrapped tightly around her like she did her mother. She was quiet while she stared at the floor. My heart sank deeper as my eyes welled with tears, and they fell down my face.

"Suga time to go, baby. You're going home with me. Don't worry about any of your things. We can come back to get them or replace them," I said.

I stood there quietly as I watched her sniffle while lying in Mrs. Lowell's lap. We both knew that Teesa could never be replaced and that she was gone. Everyone in the room stood silently, waiting for Suga to respond. For a moment, she continued to lay on Mrs. Lowell's lap unfazed as if she were in a trance. She slowly lifted her head from Mrs. Lowell's lap, and looked at me with red swollen eyes.

"She's gone," Suga said, as she cried out to me.

"I know. The police are going to find out who did this," I responded as I rushed to comfort her.

I held her arm and assisted her to her feet. Mrs. Lowell stood up slowly with stiff legs from holding the weight of Suga's pain. We walked out to the car holding each other tightly. The crowd was still assembled outside as cameras flashed. I rushed to get Suga away from the crime scene. Suddenly, she stood still as the coroner wheeled her mother out in a black body bag.

"Suga, let's go," I said. I directed her to my car. "Baby, it's time to go." I tried to pull her away; she didn't move.

"No!" she screamed as she collapsed into my arms.

The tears flowed down my face as I realized this would be a long road for her. I picked her up like I did when she was a little girl and carried her to the car. I knew that was not the time to fold because I had to be strong for my sister and Suga. By the time I made it to the car, my chest was heavy with pain that I could no longer contain. I laid her on the

SNOOK

back seat of the car. The echo from the door sent a piercing pain through my stomach that raced up to my chest. I fell to my knees on the pavement and wept loudly. I wept for Teesa and Suga. I couldn't believe someone murdered my baby sister. The anger was unbearable, and someone had to pay.

CHAPTER 3

Linwood

I t was early in the morning in the maximum security prison. That was where I'd lived for the past several months. The lights were still out, and the air was cool. All that was heard were a few coughs and sneezes through the dimmed halls. I was up early as usual, and performing my daily routine of pushups and crunches.

"Why do you get up so early to exercise? Why not just work out in the gym like the rest of us?" Lamar asked as he lay on the bottom bunk.

He'd been my cellmate for the past week, and was new to the facility.

"I'm not like everyone else," I replied as I counted out my reps. "The white man unlocks the doors to the gym, and you're the first one in there exercising the wrong muscles. You should be educating yourself, spending your time trying to get out, and planning your survival when you do," I said sternly.

I didn't like to be questioned by the young dudes or anyone else for that matter. Stopping in the middle of my set, I addressed Lamar.

"I'm just trying to do my time and go home to my family," I said, as I wiped the sweat from my forehead.

"So, what did you do to land yourself in here?" Lamar asked, scratching his head.

"What the hell did you do?"

"Man, I got a body. You know how that goes," Lamar said while shrugging his shoulders.

"You were charged with murder for killing your boyfriend, right?" I leaned against the bunk.

Lamar sat up quickly.

"Naw man, that ain't what happened," Lamar said defensively. "Yeah, I knew him from around the way. We were locked up in the county together, and he went back and told my folks that I got down while we were in. That shit wasn't true, and I had to handle that shit. You would've done the same thing," he added.

"No. I wouldn't have been in that situation."

"So you sayin' in all the time you've been here you ain't ever—"

Interrupting him, I leaped on top of Lamar and placed my hand around his neck with my knee in his side.

"Don't question me young blood. I know why you're here. You killed your boyfriend, and I don't condone nor do I tolerate that shit. I'm a man here and out there," I said through clenched teeth.

Lamar's face turned red from the air being choked out of him. He clawed at my hands, but didn't have the strength to pry my fingers away. I unleashed my grip from around his neck and let him take in air. I didn't plan on killing him. The point was to let him know that I could. I kept my knee in his side, just in case he tried me after I released my grip. When I felt that Lamar wasn't a threat, I let him up. He sat up, coughed and rubbed his neck. I'd waited all week to have that conversation with him after finding out the reason for his incarceration. I was glad I finally did.

"I'm not gay," Lamar managed to say while inhaling deeply.

"I'm not your maker or your judge," I responded nonchalantly.

After my morning workout was over, I decided to finish reading a book I borrowed from another inmate.

"Mr. White, the warden would like to see you. Let's go!" the corrections officer yelled.

I looked up from my book and removed my reading glasses.

"Tell him I'm busy. I'll see him when I'm done," I replied.

"No, now! I don't have time for this shit today. Just get your ass up!"

Since I was in a good mood, I decided to let the corrections officer slide. Under normal circumstances, the officer would've had a visit to the infirmary. I hoped that there was good news about my appeal, and I wouldn't let anything or anyone ruin my day.

"Step forward and place your hands behind your back," the corrections officer demanded.

I knew the routine, so I followed the officer's instructions. The door slid open as I watched him place the shackles on my ankles. I walked down the dull green hallway as I was led to the warden's office. I stood in front of the warden's desk and waited for him to get off of the phone. The office was like the rest of the place, dry and dull. There was an extensive collection of books on the bookshelves that lined the walls. I would've loved to have a day to read some of the law books in the warden's collection. He quickly ended the conversation and focused his attention on me.

"You wanted to see me?" I asked with a calm tone.

"Yes, Mr. White. I have some bad news to tell you. Please, take a seat," the warden said. He pointed towards the chair in front of his desk.

"I'm good. What's up?"

I wanted to know what the bad news was and beating around the bush wasn't my style. The solemn look on the warden's face made me take a seat.

"I just received a call from your brother. There has been a death in your family. Teesa Johnson passed away yesterday. I'm sorry for your loss. There are resources in place to help you get through this. Unfortunately, you will not be permitted to attend the funeral services. It's my understanding that she's not an immediate family member. This is always hard, and I'm here to do all that I can for you and your family."

The warden sat quietly as he waited for me to respond.

"Mr. White, are you okay?"

The room seemed smaller, and the air was minimal.

As I gritted my teeth, I asked, "Is that all?"

I stood tall and pretended that my heart wasn't just

ripped out and dissected in front of me. My knees wobbled as a sense of emptiness came over me.

"What did they say about my daughter? Is she all right?" I had more questions to ask.

How did she die? Did someone kill her and why? Being the man that I am, he can't see me fold. I guess that's pride for you, I thought.

"There was no information given regarding a child. If I find out anything else, I will be sure to let you know. Again, I'm sorry for your loss. Officer, please escort him back to his cell," the warden said over the intercom. When the corrections officer entered, I felt as though cement was on my legs.

As I walked back to my cell, I tried to hold it together. I loved Teesa and my daughter with all of my heart. Being incarcerated made me powerless as to what went on outside of the walls that surrounded me. It made me feel weak and less than a man. The tears were ready and waited on an introduction. When I stepped back into my cell reality could no longer be denied. The tears came like a storm, and my heart cried out for Teesa and Suga.

I mourned for three days and refused to leave my cell to bathe or eat. On the fourth day, they had to physically remove me from my cell. I bit off an ear, broke a nose, and literally fucked up four corrections officers as they entered my cell. The corrections officers had to come in with gear ready for battle. They sprayed mace, which was the only way they could take me down. I was moved to a single cell where I was placed on suicide watch.

The time I spent in solitary gave me a chance to think

about life and my past mistakes. I was serving time for money laundering, but I was also being punished for my hidden sins. I was a well-respected business owner, but also a ringleader of thieves. I owned a successful lounge that hosted several upscale corporate functions. Teesa and I met at the lounge one night and instantly fell in love. She was the most beautiful woman in the lounge that night. Women were around all the time, but Teesa was in a class of her own. She took my breath away. Sometimes I wasn't sure if she loved me or loved the things I provided for her.

I was a provider, and my family wanted for nothing. I rubbed elbows with politicians, corporate business owners, and a few celebrities. The same men and women whose corporate functions I set up and organized also hired me to make false insurance claims on stolen goods. I was the brains behind the operation. Careful not to get my hands dirty, I planned each job carefully. I trusted a few silent investors, but still managed to form a small group of thieves. They would break into the homes and businesses of my crooked clients and take what was requested to be stolen. The owners would file their insurance claims and pay me a fee for my services. I'd treat the payments as services for the lounge. My unethical business practices eventually caught the attention of the Internal Revenue Service.

Business was good for many years until one of my partners, Trey, felt that he was tired of walking in my shadow. My swagger was like no other, and many envied my life. When I walked into a room, my presence captivated everyone around me.

Trey was young, but I knew that he had what it took to run the operation. The lounge alone took in more than enough money, but there was always money to be made, and I didn't mind making it. I took Trey under my wing and showed him the ropes. I showed him how to run my operation without getting caught up. Trey was like a sponge and took it all in. I trusted and treated him like a son. Loyalty was definitely a concern, and since I trusted no one, I kept Trey closest to me for that reason. It wasn't long before I found out he did his own jobs behind my back. It was my business to know every move he made. I played the blind eye. Soon after, he was arrested for possession of stolen goods and used me as his get out of jail free card.

CHAPTER 4

Suga

oving in with my Uncle Redd and Alyssa was a difficult and emotional transition. My uncle made sure I was comfortable. Being my mother's brother, he was the only person willing to take me in. Grandma Johnson needed around the clock care and was too ill to take care of me. My Aunt Sable suddenly disappeared shortly after the funeral. She didn't talk to the family very often. There were a few great aunts and cousins, but no one wanted the responsibility of taking care of me, and they didn't hide their feelings about it.

At the funeral, I overheard a great aunt say, "I don't have time for no fast ass little girl. You know she was giving Teesa all sorts of problems behind them boys."

That was far from the truth. I had boys after me, but I wasn't interested in dating. My mother didn't allow me to talk to boys on the phone.

She'd tell me, *"There is plenty of time for that."*

All she wanted me to do was go to school and make good grades. So I didn't allow boys to take my mind off of my studies. Disappointing my mother was not an option. Furthermore, I didn't want to become a teenage mother like some of the girls I went to school with. I certainly didn't want to lose my flattering figure. It seemed as though everyone returned from summer break pregnant.

Instead of family and friends gathering to celebrate my mother's life, they were busy whispering not only about how she died, but who was to blame. One of the many rumors about her death was that my father had her killed. Others summed it up to just an overdose. One thing was for sure I knew my mom wasn't a junkie. I overheard my uncle saying that it was a heroin overdose. She may have enjoyed a few lines of cocaine every now and then, but she didn't use heroin.

Uncle Redd took my mother's death hard like most of the people that were close to her. No one took it as hard as I did.

It took me some time to get settled in my new environment. Adjusting to a new school was difficult. I was no longer living in the city. I thought the suburbs were quiet and boring. The city was always jumping. That was where all of the action took place. The county made me feel disconnected from the life I knew and loved. Uncle Redd tried to assure me that it was no different from the city, and it was just that there were better communities and school systems.

For the first few weeks after the funeral, I stayed in my room. I could barely eat or sleep from the repeated nightmares of seeing my mom's lifeless body. Uncle Redd had to force me to eat. I could tell he wanted to ask questions about my mother's death. He'd strike up a conversation about her and quickly change the subject. I guess he didn't want to force me to relive the tragedy. He'd stare at me at times as though he wanted to ask me something, but was afraid.

"Suga, it's been long enough. You can't stay cooped up in this room," Uncle Redd said, as he opened the blinds.

He sat down at the foot of the bed and looked at me solemnly.

"I don't want to go anywhere, and I don't want to see anyone," I mumbled from underneath the covers.

"I tell you what, let's make a deal. If you come out of your room and eat dinner with the family, you can earn yourself a visit to the mall. I'll let you pick out a whole new wardrobe," he offered.

He had my attention.

"Can I pick out all of my clothes?"

"Of course you can. I know you're tired of wearing your aunt's hand me downs," he replied while laughing.

"You got that right! No offense," I said, mustering up laughter.

That was the first time I had laughed since my mother's death. It felt good to share a laugh with my uncle.

"I don't know what else to do, Suga. I don't think it's right that I had to bribe you to get out of this funk. Don't let this be the way that you handle your problems in life. Don't make me regret this, you hear me?" he asked sternly.

I started a new life. The catch was that I had to come out of my room during the day, spend time with the family, and eat at the dinner table. Uncle Redd felt that would help me out of my depression, and he was right.

I wasn't excited about preparing for school. It was my junior year. I wasn't interested in my classmates, and I could've cared less about extracurricular activities. I would've liked to be back in the city attending my previous school with my friends, but I knew I didn't have a choice. With no intentions on making new friends, I isolated myself and refused to expose the hidden pain seemed to work best for me. Remaining focused on my goal to finish high school was all I wanted, as I'd promised my mother.

Uncle Redd laid down the rules and expectations. He made it clear that he wouldn't tolerate defiant behavior or below standard grades. If I disobeyed him, he'd stop providing me with a weekly allowance. Don't think I didn't earn it. My chores were a part of the rules, so I agreed with the intentions of not letting anything or anyone get in the way of my money.

We pulled in front of the school on the first day, and it didn't look much different from my last school other than the beautiful landscaping that surrounded the brick building.

Being a new student, I had to meet with the school's administrator. I sat in the front office waiting to be called to the back. Pictures of previous students, both athletic and professional, hung on the off-white painted walls. The traffic of students and faculty heavily flowed in and out of the office. A red headed, petite woman wearing glasses stood at the receptionist desk and greeted the students.

"Suga Johnson," she called.

SNOOK

"Yes, that's me," I said, standing to my feet.

"Good morning. Follow me, please," she said, leading me down a narrow hallway to her office.

"Suga, I'm Mrs. Hunter. I have reviewed your transcripts, and they're remarkable. You were a straight-A student and class president at your last school," she said while flipping through my file. "Your uncle must be very proud and I'm sorry to hear about your mother. I think you won't have any problems adjusting here," Mrs. Hunter added.

"Yes, he is very proud of me," I said, giving her a fake smile.

All I wanted was my class schedule so that I could get the day started.

"You should think about extracurricular activities. It looks good on your college applications and allows you to meet some of your new classmates," she said. She pulled her glasses down on her nose. "Since you're coming into the middle of the school year that would be good for you."

I looked at Mrs. Hunter and tried to pretend she wasn't getting on my nerves.

"I don't want to be late to class considering this is my first day. I want to make a good first impression," I said, laying it on thick.

I grabbed my book bag from the floor, my class schedule from her desk, and headed towards the door. As I opened the door, Mrs. Hunter stopped me.

"Suga if you ever need anything my door is always open, okay? Enjoy your day."

"You do the same," I responded, as I closed the door behind me.

The bell rung and the hallways were almost clear. There were a few tardy stragglers who lofted around aimlessly. From what I could tell, it seemed the students were anxious to be in class. Where I'm from, there were more people in the hallway than in the classroom. The classrooms were as nice as the outside of the school. The floors were buffed brightly, which allowed me to see my reflection.

If the cafeteria is as clean as the rest of the school, I might eat lunch here, I thought.

As I walked down the hallway, I looked up at the classroom numbers above each door one by one. I checked them against my class schedule. The last thing I needed was to walk into the wrong class. Once I confirmed that I was at the right door, I took a deep breath and opened the heavy door. I was the last one to make it into English class, so the teacher didn't acknowledge the squeaky door. She gave me a quick glance as I handed her my card with my information on it. I quickly scanned the room for an empty seat. At my previous school, the seats in the back were always the first to fill. In this class, the only seats available were in the back of the classroom.

"Take a seat," the teacher said, after finally looking up from the stack of papers on her desk.

I quickly took a seat beside a girl named Kendra. I knew her name from the large necklace that read *Kendra* around her neck. I noticed she didn't look my way when I sat beside her. *Bitch,* I thought. The teacher took attendance and called off each student's name. When I didn't hear my name called, I raised my hand.

"Yes," the teacher said rudely.

"You didn't call my name. I'm Suga," I said.

"I have you accounted for. I knew you were here because of your tardiness to my class. By the way, tardiness will not be tolerated, Suga," she said with the attitude as most teachers that were over worked and under paid.

Yeah, whatever, I see this is going to be a long school year, I thought.

Kendra leaned over and whispered, "She's a bitch, but don't worry about her. She does that to all of us."

I smiled and introduced myself, "I'm Suga."

"My name is Kendra. Suga, huh? That's different, but I like it," Kendra said with a smile.

"I like that bag," I said.

I took a mental note that my new friend's bag was a fake, but a good one. I didn't want to call her out just yet so I pretended not to notice.

"Yeah, it was a gift. I see you have one too," she said, giving me the side eye.

We both had the same Louis Vuitton bag. Kendra probably passed hers off for months, but then I show up carrying the real thing. I'm sure she felt like tucking and hiding inside the one that she'd passed off for the real thing.

"I see you, girl, coming in here all fancy," she said while checking me out.

After class, we agreed to eat lunch together. Besides shopping and fashion, we realized that we had more in common than what we could've imagined. Although we were different in some aspects, we instantly bonded. It felt good to have an ally.

It was clear that I was the eye candy in the school. I was sure it was because I was new to the school, which made me a strong competitor to the once most popular girl in school. It was rumored that the guys placed bets on who would be the first to have sex with me. Many attempted to get my phone number but were unsuccessful. Kendra was no longer most wanted, and the more I grew to know her I realized how much she really hated it. Drawing most of the attention when we walked down the hall, Kendra was envious. Little did I know that her envy would ultimately destroy her. It was difficult for her to be the one who always received the attention, and then become an afterthought.

We mirrored each other in a lot of our qualities, but I was the most natural. I had long dark hair, and Kendra wore weave. I had long natural nails, and Kendra wore false tips. With the love of designer handbags and clothes, I was the only one who could afford the real thing. However, none of that mattered because she was just what I needed, a friend. Our friendship became inseparable.

CHAPTER 5

Kendra

After meeting Suga, she challenged me to step up my game. I couldn't look like her sidekick. Although, I thankfully accepted, it didn't help that Suga gave me her hand me downs. She even gave me one of her Chanel handbags. I appreciated it, but couldn't help but feel that Suga felt sorry for me. I loved her like a sister, but envied her easy-going lifestyle. Like my grandmother used to say, *"If you can't beat them, join them."*

Our friendship helped keep our minds off of our circumstances. With her mother dead and her father behind bars, Suga often spoke about how much she missed and longed for her mother. Her Uncle Redd was good to her and did all he could, but there was nothing he could do to replace her parents.

I was someone who she could share her feelings with. She reciprocated the friendship and allowed me to share my experiences as well. She was someone I could share everything with, and I did.

I told Suga about the time I was raped when I spent the night over my friend Laura's house. Spending the night over Laura's was something I often did. Laura's mother had a twenty-two year old boyfriend named Lee. He was extra friendly with us and often made me feel uncomfortable. Laura avoided him as much as she could and warned me to do the same. He told us how cute we were and would stick his tongue out at us seductively.

One particular night, Laura's mother got drunk and passed out on the living room sofa. Lee was still up drinking and smoking weed. We'd been asleep for hours, and I woke up in the wee hours of the night to go to the bathroom. I wandered out into the hall with my eyes half shut. I knew my way around the house in the dark because I'd been there several times. Still sleepy, I sat on the toilet and closed my eyes as my bladder drained. When finished, I was startled by a turn of the door knob.

"I'm in here!" I called out.

Realizing that I'd forgotten to lock the door, I tried to reach to turn the lock. The door slowly opened, and Lee stood in the doorway naked. He reeked of liquor and smoke that lingered in the air. I looked at him oddly as I reached down to pull up my pajama pants. My heart raced. I was unaware of what he wanted, but I wasn't trying to stick around to find out.

"Where do you think you're going?" Lee asked with drunken lust in his eyes as he stepped into the bathroom.

SNOOK

"Get out of here!" I yelled.

I stood to my feet while holding my pants tightly around my waist.

I tried to leave the bathroom, but Lee blocked me from the doorway. Trying to push him out of the way, I was disgusted by his nakedness with every touch. He shoved me back into the bathroom, then closed and locked the door.

"Help me!" I screamed, as he punched me in the mouth.

"Shut up! If you scream again, I will kill you!" Lee said, as he held his hand over my mouth.

With the fear that he would kill me, I cried silently. I felt my mouth swell as the salty taste of blood ran into my mouth. I wanted to fight back but was afraid of what he might do next. He reached into the shower and turned on the water full blast. The sound of the shower muffled my cries. At that point, I knew what would take place after that.

The next morning, Laura found me passed out on the bathroom floor. She knew what happened because the same thing had happened to her many times before. She woke me up and told me to go to her bedroom and wait for her.

Laura cleaned the bathroom and scrubbed away my innocence that Lee had stolen, which was dried up on the floor. She cried and scrubbed as hard as she could as her own experiences with Lee replayed in her mind.

She ran me a hot bath just as Lee did for her. When she returned to the bedroom, she found me in the corner shaking like a damaged mess.

"It's all right. I ran you a hot bath. That always makes me feel better," Laura said, as she stroked my hair and wiped my tears.

"He hurt me, Laura," I said through tears. "I have to tell your mom so she can call the police," I cried.

"No, please don't. He will kill us," Laura said frightened.

"What? He raped me! Look what he did to me," I said while pointing to my bruised face.

"I'm sorry this happened to you. He did the same thing to me," Laura said, as she dropped her head with regret.

It was at that moment I knew this was an argument that I couldn't win. The dysfunction that Laura created made her think that what Lee did to us was okay. I wanted to get out of there as fast as I could and never look back.

Laura convinced me to get into the bathtub. I soaked my sore body in the hot bath for an hour. I wanted the last twenty-four hours to go down the drain with the bath water. Afterward, I got dressed and went home, never to discuss that night again. I told my mother that Laura and I had gotten into a fight and were no longer friends. I had no plans of ever going back to her house and vowed never to tell anyone about the rape.

I didn't know why Suga wasn't interested in boys, and she questioned my practices with them. After she had found out about the rape, Suga understood me better. She still didn't approve of my ways but tried to encourage me and didn't judge me. She felt that the rape was the reason I was so promiscuous.

CHAPTER 6

Suga

*A*fter graduating high school, it was time to focus on college. I applied to a few colleges but was only interested in one. Every day I was the first to the mailbox. I was looking for my acceptance letter and finally one day it came. I tore into the letter as my nerves raced.

"Uncle Redd, Uncle Redd, I got in!" I screamed through the house. "I'm going to V.C.U. School of Business," I yelled excitedly.

Virginia Commonwealth University offered one of the best business programs. I called out to Uncle Redd again with no answer. I froze in place while caught up with excitement. I realized that the front door was opened when I came in. A queasy feeling came over me as déjà vu played in my head. Something was wrong. As I tiptoed down the hall, I could hear whispers coming from the kitchen. Fear crawled up my spine and fluttered all over my body. The unexpected stalked me like the dark spirit that took my mother away. As I quietly crept toward the kitchen, I heard a chair slide across the kitchen floor.

Just when my thoughts were telling me to turn around and run back out of the door, Uncle Redd jumped out and yelled, "Congratulations! My baby is off to college!"

"Shit!" I screamed out, as I almost pissed my pants.

My grandmother, cousins, aunt, and friends were all there in the kitchen to greet me. Everyone laughed at my reaction to the surprise. Trying to get over the fear that took over my body, it was difficult to comprehend what happened. Suddenly, I felt lightheaded and everything faded to black. I fainted. I woke up with everyone standing over me.

As I came to, the faint vision that stood over me looked like my mother. I soon realized it was my Aunt Sable, my mom's identical twin sister. When I was younger, it was difficult to tell the two apart. I eventually found a special feature that helped me to identify who was who.

"Suga, wake up baby," my Aunt Sable said, as she gently rubbed my head and fanned me.

Although their physical appearances were similar, they had totally different personalities. Aunt Sable had a small mole above her top lip. I remember my mom sharing how they were inseparable growing up. During their teen years, they grew apart fast and chose different paths in life.

For a moment, Aunt Sable provided a sense of security that only a mother could give. That was something I hadn't felt in a long time. There was an instant connection between us. For a moment, I thought I woke up from a bad dream, and my mother was alive. That's how eerie the feeling was.

"Come on baby, drink this," Aunt Sable ordered as she put the cup to my mouth. "Now, why are you fainting on the biggest day of your life?" she asked.

I noticed her big framed dark shades that covered her entire face. She handed me the glass of water and said very little. I grabbed the glass from her and enjoyed the moment. I was happy to see Aunt Sable. She was the closest thing to my mother. No one had seen her since my mom's funeral. Her disappearance was suspicious. We all knew she moved to North Carolina right after the funeral, and she rarely visited. She'd call and check on me periodically. She kept her distance as if she believed her presence would be too painful for the family. We believed that was her way of coping with the death of her twin. It was understood considering how close the two of them were so no one pressured her. I gave quick glances at her, noticing how much she mirrored my mother.

"I'm so sorry. I don't know what happened," I said as I got up off of the floor. "Let me get cleaned up so we can party."

I was embarrassed as I walked out of the kitchen and to my room. While changing my clothes, I quickly became excited about my surprise party. All of my family came to support me. My mother not being there to celebrate with me hurt the most.

"Come on, Suga, your friends are here," Uncle Redd said. He knocked on the bedroom door.

"I'm ready!" I yelled out.

The night was full of fun and excitement. Everyone expressed how proud they were of me and my accomplishments. Although I would leave to attend college, I wouldn't be too far from my loved ones. Being closer to my family had its benefits. I knew it was less expensive for in-state tuition. I didn't want to be a burden on Uncle Redd and Alyssa anymore. I wanted my independence, so I opted to live on campus. I knew if it didn't work out, he would be more than happy to welcome me back home.

I shook off the thoughts of Aunt Sable that nagged me. I just assumed I was trying to find a substitute for my mother. As the night came to an end, I realized that my life was finally going in the right direction.

"Hey Suga, there are a few cards and gifts you haven't opened yet," Uncle Redd said, as he looked through the cards. "I don't know what could top this, a brand new Honda Accord!" he said, waving a set of keys in the air.

"Oh my God! Oh my God! I can't believe it!" I said excitedly. "Uncle Redd you got me a new car!" I said, jumping up and down.

I grabbed the keys and ran out to the garage. There it was, a black Honda Accord. It was the exact one I wanted.

"Go ahead and get in. Check it out, Suga," he said proudly.

I fought back tears. After several seconds, I looked at Uncle Redd as I watched tears run down his cheeks. He watched me grovel over the new car.

"Suga, a package came for you this morning. There wasn't a return address, but it was addressed to you," he said.

SNOOK

"Who would send me something without a return address? Did you open it?" I asked.

He handed me the package that he held in his hands.

"No, but I have my suspicions about it. Go on an open it," he ordered. He walked out of the garage to give me privacy. "Call me if you need me."

I looked at the package puzzled with suspicion and curiosity. As I slowly opened it, a small key fell out onto my lap. I held the key up and examined it. It was small like one used on a padlock. I continued to rip open the rest of the package and noticed there was a handwritten letter inside. A smaller package was wrapped tightly in the bottom of the box. I opened the letter first and noticed the bad handwriting.

Dear Suga,

I know you don't really know me anymore, but I'm your father. I know I've been gone for a long time, and I wasn't there for you and your mother. I miss her every day, and I'm sorry you had to go through that alone. She was the love of my life, and I know no one misses her more than you. I want you to know that I've always loved you and always will. Circumstance has kept me away, and one day you will understand what that is. I want you to trust no one, believe nothing you can't see, and most of all keep this key close to your heart. I love you.

Your father,
Linwood

Tears fell onto the paper, making the ink run down the paper. It wasn't because I finally heard from my long lost father, but the nerve he had to choose that day of all days to contact me. I was hurt and angry at the same time.

Why hasn't he tried to reach me before? How can you love me, and you're not here for me? Why now? I thought.

I wanted to throw the package and letter into the trash but decided to see what else was sent. I opened the small package and found four thousand dollars. In shock, I held the money in my hands as it made me warm on the inside.

Money always made me feel good, but that amount of money in cash made me tingle in places that it shouldn't have. I'd never seen or held that much money in my life. I tucked the money back in the envelope and ripped the letter to shreds. I had big plans for the four thousand dollars that had instantly fallen into my lap. The key, on the other hand, was something else. I examined it and wondered the story it held?

What was so important about the key? Well, if it leads to more money than I'd better keep it safe, I thought.

I looked in the mirror, and I admired the new diamond necklace Uncle Redd gave me.

I was spoiled, and there was no doubt about that. Uncle Redd believed the only way to keep me happy was to buy me expensive gifts and take me on weekly shopping sprees. It did appear that I was happier when I had money, a designer bag, and the latest clothes and shoes. Deep down inside, we knew it was a huge mistake, but I knew he didn't know what else to do at the time. Over time, Uncle Redd mentioned that he saw a change in me that scared him. I loved money so much that it seemed to dictate how I felt about myself. He told me that he prayed that eventually I would realize my worth.

Shortly after I graduated, I met the love of my life, Marlon. I fell in love with Marlon the very first time I laid eyes on him. One night Kendra invited me to the movies with her and her boyfriend, Dee. Dee brought along his friend, Marlon. My initial plan was to ignore Marlon and enjoy the movie. The theater was the place to hang out and make out on Saturday nights. At least it was for the young people.

Kendra and I lied so that we could hang out the entire weekend. I told Uncle Redd we were going to the movies with friends and then to Kendra's house afterward and Kendra told her mom that she would be at my house. She planned to hang out and go to the hotel with Dee afterward. I went along for the ride. While we walked along the road that led to the movie theater, I could tell that Kendra was very excited by the big Kool-Aid smile on her face.

"Girl, I can't wait to see him. I haven't had that dick for over a week now," Kendra said, grinning from ear to ear. "Stop acting like you don't want a man like him." She laughed.

"Please. Don't try to hook me up with his ugly ass friend, either. I'm just helping you out," I said.

"That's what you say now, but wait until you see him," Kendra said, giving me a wink.

"See who? Girl, I've told your ass. Don't play with me. I

will turn my ass around and go right back home," I said, crossing my arms in front of me.

Kendra looked at me and laughed, "Stop being a bitch all the time."

We both laughed.

We finally made it to the theater. Once inside, we waited in the long line to order buttered popcorn and our drinks.

"Hey, Marlon," Kendra said, as she reached her arms out to hug him.

I turned and saw my future flash before my eyes. Marlon had more swag than all of the men in the theater put together. His ice was ridiculous, which put me in a trance.

"What's up?" Marlon asked me.

Speechless, I looked at him with dreamy eyes.

"Oh hello… I'm sorry, I'm Suga," I said, as I reached out my hand.

He stimulated me. I knew money when I saw it, and it was a tingle that wouldn't stop. I tried to play it cool, but I couldn't hide my inexperience.

As pretty as I was, at the ripe age of eighteen, I'd never had a boyfriend. The guys at school didn't have the money it took to catch my attention. Besides, I was focused on my studies and the latest fashion trends. Other times I hid my depression with a smile on my face. I'd been on and off of anti-depressants to help with nightmares and anxiety. Although they were prescribed, I didn't take the Xanax daily as the doctor advised. I used my judgment of what I needed. I didn't want to become dependent on medication to function, so I took them when I felt the need to *feel better* or when I felt anxiety. I learned quickly that the pills were worth more to me by selling them to my classmates. They'd buy them like candy and of all nights with a theater full of teenagers I was out of pills.

Kendra stood back and watched me work. After ordering buttered popcorn and a Pepsi, we headed inside the theater. The lights were still on as we looked for seats. The sticky floors made noise as we made our way down the aisle. A few people recognized Marlon and Dee and broke their necks to speak to them.

I took notice of how Marlon's presence commanded respect. He must've been someone special for people to want his attention. That made the situation even sweeter.

Who is he? Whoever he is, he's mine now, I thought.

I wondered, and I couldn't wait to ask Kendra. I knew I was out of my element. Flirting with a guy was something I'd never done before. I didn't want to try too hard, so I decided to go with the flow. Besides, I knew nothing about him except his name. He looked older than the high school guys, so I had to be careful not to come across as immature. He was laid back and seemed very quiet. There wasn't much conversation between the two of us during the movie, but my body was having a private conversation of its own. The silence between us gave me time to plan how I would let him know that I was feeling him.

The closer we came to the end of the movie the more nervous I became. I wanted to get some air and have Kendra fill in the blanks.

"Kendra, let's go to the restroom," I whispered as I leaned over to her.

"Girl, you go. I'm cool," Kendra said between passionate kisses with Dee.

I grabbed her arm and pulled her up.

"Okay, damn! I'm coming," she said, yanking her arm from me.

We both put on a smile and excused ourselves.

"What's wrong, Suga? Why did you grab me up like that? Have you been taking your medicine?" Kendra asked, as she surveyed me cautiously.

At that point, I was sweaty and breathing heavily.

"Come on, Suga, let's get some air," she said.

She wrapped her arms around me and led me to the doors. Trying to get my breathing under control, Kendra rubbed my back like she always did during a panic attack.

"Girl, when is this going to stop? I'm tired of these attacks controlling my life. It's embarrassing. I thought I was going to faint. Who wants to be with a nut job like me?" I asked tearfully.

"What happened? Did Marlon do something?" Kendra asked.

"No, it's me. I think I like him," I admitted.

"Ok, so what's the problem? I know it's a first, and you will have many of them. You're going to have to suck that shit up, girl. I know this is new to you, but you got this. You always had it," Kendra said, as she rubbed her fingers through my hair. "You don't have to try too hard. You're naturally beautiful and have a great personality. It's time to get yourself out there. Enjoy life!" she said, as she smiled with excitement. "Now come on and get your man. I knew you'd like him. He's got money, too, girl!"

SNOOK

"So, you think I just want him for his money?" I asked as I continued to fan myself. "I could really like him, you know? Maybe even be his wife one day," I added, knowing that was too premature, but I could see it.

"Yes, I do. The same way you liked that new Louis Vuitton bag your uncle just bought you," she replied as we both laughed.

The security officer walked over and asked if we were patrons. We were instructed to return to the theater or leave the property. When we got back to our seats, the guys were laughing at a scene in the movie.

"I thought you left me," Marlon whispered into my ear.

His warm breath and cologne were like aphrodisiacs and sending signals to the brain between my legs.

"I would never leave you," I replied while smiling.

"I hope not," Marlon flirted back.

That night sealed our fate.

Instead of heading to the hotel as planned, we headed home. There was a change of plans when Dee decided that money was more important than spending time with Kendra. Marlon and I exchanged phone numbers and promised to keep in contact. I was happy that Kendra talked me into going to the movies with her and Dee. The average guy never caught my attention, but Marlon was a man. I decided it was time for me to get my feet wet and let the rest fall into place. He appeared to have it all together and could provide some of the things that I needed to be happy. Before leaving, Marlon gave me a hug that gave me chills. I held on tight not wanting to let him go. His body felt so damn good, and our bodies fit perfectly.

"Get a room you two," Kendra said jokingly.

She was surprised by my openness to Marlon. She never saw me talk to a guy longer than five minutes let alone hug one.

"Let my girl breathe! Damn!" Kendra said, as she laughed at us cuddling.

"Bring your ass over here," Dee said, as he winked at Kendra. "Why are you worrying about them?" he asked while sharing a passionate kiss with Kendra. "Marlon! We got to go, man," he yelled.

While Marlon held onto me, he whispered in my ear, "What will it take for you to be my queen?"

"A king's ransom," I replied.

I looked him in his eyes, meaning every word. Although, he made me melt, money was the key to my happiness. The only way he could have me was to have plenty of it.

"Now you sound like all of the rest of these gold digging chicks," Marlon said, as he backed away from me. "I thought you were different."

I'm sure he wondered if I was really worth the trouble.

Was he willing to do whatever it took to keep me laced in the finer things in life?

"I'm Suga. Baby, I know my worth," I said, as the butterflies inside of me finally subsided. "I know what I want, and that's you. I'm not like these dumb chicks. I won't bargain. I'm not afraid to tell you what I want and need. I was raised that a man should come correct or don't come at all," I said without hesitation.

"That's what's up. I got you. Just give me some time, and

I'm going to give you everything your heart desires. I got plans for us," Marlon said confidently.

"So do I, but I'm going to college in the fall. I plan on starting my own business one day."

"I recently graduated from college."

I was impressed and knew for sure he was older. I needed to know his plans.

"Graduated from where? You don't look like a college guy to me."

He didn't look like a college guy, but he didn't appear to be like the rest of the guys on the streets that seemed to have a one-way ticket to prison.

"Oh, so I look dumb or something? Looks can be deceiving. Gone ahead with that shit," he said brushing me off. "You have a lot to learn, little girl. I'm not like the rest of these guys out here," he said.

I reminded him once again of how immature I was.

"That's the problem with females. They don't know a good man when he's standing right in front of them. Look shorty, me and Dee got to get this paper," he said.

He kissed me on the forehead as he gradually moved down to my lips. I melted as his soft lips swallowed mine.

I just had my first kiss. I'm going to marry this man one day, I thought.

On the way home, I checked my pocket to make sure that his number was still there. The worse thing that could've happened was for his number to fall out, and I'd have to ask Kendra to get it again.

Two days passed before I broke down and called Marlon. I didn't want him to think I was desperate since desperation didn't look good on me. I tried to occupy myself and not think about him. I hoped he thought about me as much as I did of him. Dialing his number was scary. When the phone rung, I thought I would pee my pants.

"Hello?" he answered.

"Hello, may I speak to Marlon?" I asked in my sexiest voice.

"What's up, Suga?" Marlon asked.

Stumped, I sat on the phone in silence. I didn't expect him to recognize my voice.

"How did you know it was me?" I asked.

"You're the only one that has this number. What took you so long to call me?"

"I've been busy," I said nonchalantly. "Why are you starting out telling lies? If that's your way of trying to tell me that I'm the only one, you can save it. I'm sure you have plenty of girls after you. Don't lie."

"All I meant was that you were the only one with this number. I recently changed my number because of the girls you're referring to."

I felt small and once again inexperienced. I'd watched Kendra talk to guys on the phone all the time. I thought I had soaked in all of her experience, but this conversation proved me wrong. I had to abort the Kendra plan and come up with one of my own. Taking the lead in the conversation,

SNOOK

Marlon knew how to make me feel comfortable. Before I knew it, it was almost midnight before I yawned on the phone. Neither one of us wanted to get off of the phone, so we talked until we both dozed off.

The next morning, I woke up to the sound of the alarm with the cordless phone stuck to the side of my face. I smiled thinking about Marlon. Thinking of him made the butterflies in my stomach flutter. I wanted to spend every waking minute with him, but I knew that was impossible. I wanted to keep my promise to my mother. School was first, and then men however Marlon was an exception. I'd finish school and have my man by any means necessary.

For the remainder of the summer, we spent every weekend together. I was to leave for college in a few weeks. Marlon and I saw each other as much as we could. We even talked on the phone every night.

CHAPTER 7

Marlon

*I*n the fall semester, Suga moved into the dorms. She planned to focus so she could be home in three years instead of four. We had plans to begin our lives together. I pushed her to stay focused on her education and tried to assure her I wouldn't go anywhere. I loved the drive that she had to pursue her education, so I made sure she stayed on track. We spoke every night, and I helped with her studies. Every weekend I took her out to release the stress that came with college life. It had been a while and we hadn't even had sex. She was different, and I hoped she didn't give it to those knuckleheads on campus. I wanted to be patient, but it was damn near killing me.

While Suga was off getting her education, I took the time to work on my business plan. I had hard work ahead of me, but I had to be smart to prosper. Every dime earned had to be accounted for. I decided to take a job as an operations manager that offered a decent salary. I took on a roommate so that I could save every paycheck I earned. I deposited the checks into an account for three years. I managed to meet my goal and went into business for myself. Along the way, I developed trusted business relationships with some of the firm's biggest clients. I never missed an opportunity to network with potential clients and suppliers. My short term, three-year plan helped to plan for our future.

"Will you marry me?" I asked Suga at her college graduation party.

"Yes, baby. I'll marry you!" Suga screamed while jumping up and down with tears in her eyes.

We hadn't seen each other much over the last few months of her senior year of college. I worked long hours and knew the rewards were worth the time I put in. Since Suga graduated, I had time to build my business.

"I love you, Suga, baby," I said, sliding the custom made diamond ring onto her finger.

The ring was three carats and beautifully made just for her. She was speechless.

She admired the ring. "I've never seen a ring so beautiful. You're really serious about this, huh?"

"Yes, I'm serious about us." I kissed her on her forehead. "I knew you would be mine since the first time we met."

It sent chills down my spine from the love I felt for her. She closed her eyes as I kissed her lips softly. With all of our friends and family present, it was an amazing feeling to have them there to watch us take our relationship to the next level.

"Honey, can I talk to you about something?" Suga asked, pulling me to the side.

"What's up? Is everything all right? I hope I didn't put you on the spot."

"No, it's just that I have something to tell you. I don't know how you're going to feel about this, but you would've eventually found out. It's better that I warn you now."

"Look, you can tell me anything. Don't ever hold back anything from me," I said with an uneasy feeling. "What's up with you?"

Any time a woman says she needs to talk; it's never anything good.

"I'm a virgin and I'm glad you will be my first. You have been my first everything." She paused. "How does that make you feel? Do you still want to marry me?"

Either she's starting this thing off all wrong with unnecessary lies, or she thinks I'm crazy, I thought.

I was sure the look on my face showed true shock.

"You're not a virgin. You don't have to be a virgin for me to marry you. You're joking, right?" I asked in a confused tone.

"Hell no! I'm serious, and you're turning this into a joke. It's not funny. Why can't you believe that I haven't had sex before? I'd never had the urge to have sex until I met you." She looked away shyly. "I was afraid, so I just avoided it."

"It's cool, baby. That's even better. I'm going somewhere no man has been before." I kissed her and held her in my arms. "I love you regardless, even more now than before."

"That's why I love you."

I was skeptical and still didn't think Suga was a virgin.

SNOOK

Any man would have had her. She was too damn fine not to have received pleasure from a man. I felt honored to have her virginity if it was mine to have.

That night, we made love for the first time. I went along with the virgin story and took my time with her. Since that was the first time seeing her naked, I paid close attention to every detail of her sculptured body. I took note of every distinctive mark on her body, as my tongue caressed her body. I noticed the mole between her thighs and a birthmark on her lower back. After that night, I knew she was pure. I fell deeper in love with her. After a one-year engagement, we were married.

Suga

A year after Marlon and I were married, we owned a lucrative jewelry store. He was able to go back to college and earn a master's degree in business. After five years, we owned a chain of successful jewelry stores. With my degree in business, I took care of the accounting for the company. I'd acquired contracts with local business owners all of whom were contacts Marlon kept from the firm where he worked. We were living the good life, just the way I'd imagined it.

We owned a beautiful home, which sat on the outskirts of the City of Richmond. The house had an additional guesthouse, theater room, and an indoor pool. We often hosted parties and family gatherings. I loved showing off my home and my expensive art collection.

Most of Marlon's entertainment clientele wanted custom made necklaces, and the biggest diamond earrings that their ears could hold. Then there were some that preferred smaller more conservative pieces. From the rappers and husbands buying their mistresses the most expensive pieces they could afford, we were financially blessed.

Love was good to me. Over time the panic attacks and nightmares eventually stopped. Marlon made sure I stood out in a crowd with the latest designer clothes, handbags, shoes, and custom jewelry. He provided the best that money could buy.

"Happy anniversary, babe!" I said, pushing open his office door.

I wore the tightest black dress I could find in the closet. I stood tall in my six-inch red stilettos. Marlon loved to see me in heels. I had plans for him once I arrived at the office, but instead I found my best friend Kendra leaning over his desk. Marlon pretended to look at his computer screen. He couldn't fool a cow. He was enjoying the channel he was watching. Kendra always had a nice body. After giving birth to her daughter, she had become much curvier.

"What the hell are you doing?" I asked Kendra walking into the room.

Startled by my presence, Kendra frantically began gathering papers, causing a few to fall to the floor.

"Oh, I needed these invoices so that I could file them away. You're finished with them, right?" she asked as she straightened her clothes.

"Yes, I am. Now get out so I can fuck the shit out of my husband," I said.

Licking my painted Chanel Red lips, I felt threatened but refused to let either one of them know it. I knew Marlon found insecurity unattractive. Kendra would love to know that she was a threat to another woman. There was no way Marlon would ever be with her, no matter how hard she tried. I knew her envy made her thirsty for attention. She craved things that she couldn't have or afford.

"I guess that means you need to leave because I have some work to do," Marlon said, grinning at me.

He tilted his office chair back into a reclined position exactly where I wanted him.

"Shut up, Marlon! I'm leaving," Kendra said, glaring at him. "I love that dress, girl," she whispered as she walked past me going out of the door.

"I'm sure you do love it," I said sarcastically.

Kendra sucked her teeth and gave me the finger as she left the office. Over the years, our friendship had grown to be more competitive. No matter how hard she tried, she couldn't come close to my likeness. I'll admit that there were times I got a kick out of feeling that I was better than her. I slammed the door behind her and focused my attention on Marlon as he stroked himself through his pants.

"That's my best friend, but I don't trust her," I said. I kissed him softly. "Keep her out of this office when I'm not here. You understand me?" I shoved my erect nipple into his mouth. The floor creaked in the hallway as I looked towards the door. "I know she is not still standing out there," I said, looking for a shadow underneath the door.

All right bitch, let the games begin, I thought.

The phone rang as I teased his ears, lips, and neck with my tongue.

SNOOK

"Answer it," I said seductively.

He looked at me with a confused look on his face. I nodded my approval.

"Cole's Jewelry, how may I help you?" he said, trying to maintain a calm voice.

I slid off the dress, leaving on my red stilettos. I climbed knee first onto his two-hundred thousand dollar custom made Parnian power desk. The exotic wood and glass trimming was a seductive platform for my erotic show. It felt good to lie on top of all of that money.

"Yes, it should be here by Friday. You can come in after three o'clock," Marlon said with a quivering voice.

He piled a stack of folders on the right side of his desk, making room for the show. I swayed my hips from side to side showing off a well-defined backside.

Having his full attention, I crawled over the desk and positioned myself so that I was bent completely over the desk. I leaned into his lap head first with my ass up in the air. I unzipped his pants and reached in his boxers to pull out his thick, long penis. He slid deep into his leather chair anticipating his orgasm. My mouth opened wide enough to accept his girth, and I wrapped my lips around it.

"Yes," Marlon said, as he quickly hung up the phone.

He let out a moan. I didn't want him to get excited too soon.

While pleasing him, I made my ass cheeks move up and down with a fine arch in my back. I moved his hands away each time he reached for my ass or breast. I knew that turned him on even more.

I swallowed him, knowing that he was reaching his climax. I quickly spun around and slid on top of his penis with one swift movement. I eased down on him controlling the situation. Moving slow and steady, I tried to calm the storm that quickly brewed. I sucked his dick and rode him like the pro he'd made me. Keeping his hands and mouth at bay, he moaned loudly and squirmed in his seat. Taking control, he picked me up, laid me on top of the desk, and thrust harder inside of me, which sent waves of pleasure through my body. We collapsed on top of the desk as sweat covered us. We looked into each other's eyes.

"Get up so I can get cleaned up," I said, slapping his ass.

He lifted himself off of me, leaving me naked and exposed. The cool air quickly dried off the sweat and caused my nipples to become erect again.

"That was good, baby. If tonight is going to be anything like this, then I'm in trouble," he said, giving me a wink.

"You got that right. I have something special planned for you tonight," I said seductively.

I intentionally kept my legs spread open as I rose from the desk. He sat back and admired my center. The day before I had gotten a French wax leaving only a small strip of hair just the way he liked it. He showed his appreciation frequently by treating himself to my nectar. I slipped into our private bathroom to check the ring that I used as a birth control. He wasn't aware that I used birth control. I didn't want any children, but he did. Marlon with weak legs joined me to remove my juices from his sweaty body.

"This might be it this time. I can feel it. I don't know

why it's taking so long. The doctor said that we should be pregnant soon," I lied.

"I hope so. I'm ready to be somebody's daddy," he said excitingly.

"I know right? I can't wait to be a mother," I said, as I rubbed the cloth in between my legs.

"Where did you want to go after dinner tonight?" Marlon asked.

He walked up behind me at the sink and kissed me on the back of my neck.

"We can check out that club you told me about."

"Are you sure that's what you want to do?"

"Yes, I want to party tonight. It's our anniversary, baby, with many more to come," I said with excitement.

CHAPTER 9

Marlon

Suga and I decided to celebrate our anniversary at a newly renovated club in the city. The club was located within the long stretch of bars and nightclubs in the city's center. Unlike the city's other clubs, this one had a Miami feel to it. It stood out from the rest.

They didn't spare any expense on the décor. There was a red carpet that led straight to the front door from the valet parking. Photographers surrounded the red carpet that was blocked off with red velvet ropes. The pictures taken were sold for a fee at the picture booth inside. It made every patron feel like a rock star.

When entering the club, the waterfall sat behind bulletproof glass that formed the words *Rich City*. Crystals surrounded the bottom of the waterfall. They had the most wanted DJ on the east coast. They served the best crab legs and chicken wings in the city. On any given night, you might catch your favorite rapper or NBA player popping bottles in the V.I.P. wing of the club. The waitresses looked like models. Everyone was treated the same because the club's motto was, *Everyone's money is green.*

V.I.P. status was on the west wing where the real ballers paid to play. In that section, there were glass sliding doors and a balcony that overlooked the entire club. The room was best described as plush with all the bells and whistles. The clubs elevator led from the main floor to the V.I.P., which was operated by the biggest bouncer at the club.

It was around seven o'clock and closing time at the store. I couldn't wait to start on the anniversary plans that Suga and I had. While pulling down the front gate, I heard a car pull up. I figured it was someone coming to collect. To run a business in the downtown area, you had to pay to stay. Trey allowed me to pay a small fee since I was like family. Trey was an old friend of Suga's father, Linwood. Every month, I paid taxes with no extensions. As I got a clearer view, I noticed that it was Trey.

"What it do?" Trey asked as he leaned out of his old school Chevy with blue candy paint sitting on twenty-eight inch chrome wheels. "Where's my goddaughter?"

Trey had the ride that shined and caught the attention of everyone on the streets of the South Side. A few people in his crew had cars that were bangers, but no one's car shined like his. Trey's custom designed *South Side* medallion dazzled with canary and white diamonds on a long chain that hung from his neck, which I customized for him.

"It's our anniversary, so she is either shopping or at home getting ready for tonight," I said.

"Well, congratulations my man," Trey said.

"I didn't think that you were coming so I was getting ready to leave."

I reached into my inside jacket pocket and pulled out an envelope. The five hundred dollars was nothing to a businessman like me. I considered it to be a necessary expense. Trey would be back spending five times that in the store in no time.

CHAPTER 10

Suga

When I arrived home, I tried on my new dress at Marlon's expense. We did not only celebrate our wedding anniversary but a profitable business anniversary as well. We hadn't had children, but if it were up to him, we would have. Unfortunately, that wasn't in my plans. My selfish tendencies wouldn't dare allow me to share Marlon, let alone his money, with anyone including children. If my secret trips to the clinic didn't happen, he would've had his three children. I claimed they were lost in miscarriages to spare his feelings.

With Kendra by my side, I'd wear wigs and sunglasses to hide my identity. The way the abortions occurred was the scandalous part. I would be home for the opening act, and show him the positive pregnancy test to get him excited. Then I'd complain of stomach cramps. Marlon would fear the worst, and cater to me immediately. As I lay in bed pretending to be plagued with stomach cramps, he would endure the experience with me. Not long after, the baby was miscarried with him witnessing the entire thing. The closing act was all of the things that he did to make up for our loss. I took advantage of him as he waited on me hand and foot. He made sure that I was comfortable. He'd satisfy all of my requests including the special orders I placed with the boutique.

Marlon and I were dressed to impress. I sported a new ten-carat diamond necklace and matching five-carat diamond ring. All eyes were on us. We headed straight to the V.I.P. section where we were greeted with a bottle of Moët, which was my favorite. In the center of the table, tied with a large purple and gold bow, were a dozen of purple and yellow long stemmed roses in a crystal vase.

"Thanks, honey, they are beautiful," I said, as I sat down at the private table.

I smelled the roses and smiled at the delightful scent.

"I love this place, baby," I commented.

"It's nice isn't it? I don't know why I didn't bring you here sooner. I figured you and your girls would get around to it sooner or later," he said, as he tipped the waitress.

"Thanks for the best years of my life," Marlon said, as he kissed my hand and gazed into my eyes.

"Thank you for the best years of my life," I replied, kissing him deeply.

Marlon ordered bottle after bottle of champagne. It wasn't long before I felt the effects of the alcohol. We danced and drank the night away.

SNOOK

As the alcohol took full effect, I sat back while Marlon and another female danced. As I watched, I became angry.

"Oh, so you're going to disrespect me," I yelled over the loud music as I stumbled through the crowd.

"We are just having a good time, baby," he said nonchalantly. He smiled at me in an attempt to calm me down.

I couldn't stand the fact that someone else was getting his attention. Pissed off, I stumbled back to my seat. Marlon continued to socialize with the young lady while I watched from the bar. It was getting close to closing time. I stumbled my way to the bathroom to freshen up.

CHAPTER 11

Marlon

A s I waited for Suga to come out of the bathroom, I was stopped by one of my regular customers from the store. After several minutes and a constant look through the crowd, I realized that Suga hadn't come out of the bathroom. I was worried, and thinking that she might've gotten sick. I quickly ended the conversation and headed to the restroom to check on her. I proceeded to the back where the restrooms were located. Before entering the ladies restroom, I knocked on the door that read, *OUT OF ORDER*. That meant that the only working restroom was the men's. I instantly got a knot in my stomach. I turned towards the men's restroom. I pushed the door open. There was only one stall and the door was slightly open. I thought she might've fallen or passed out. The closer I got to the door I could hear moans. I pushed the stall door open and found Suga with her panties down around her ankles with someone between her legs. I stood in shock as I watched her being pleasured. I saw her for what she was.

SNOOK

"You bitch!" I stood there trying to control myself from killing both of them.

The man got up off his knees as we stared each other down. A bouncer jumped in front of me just as I lunged at the man. I was pulled back by someone else. I jerked away from the person, swinging wildly. The man that was eating my wife's pussy was escorted out the bathroom by another bouncer. With a smug look on his face, the man blew me off.

"Fuck you! You can have that bitch!" I yelled.

When the man was safely out of the bathroom, I was released from the bouncer's grip.

Suga, who was still noticeably intoxicated, tried to pull up her panties as she looked at me regretfully.

"I'm sorry, baby," she cried out as she struggled to straighten her dress.

I lunged towards her and pushed her back into the bathroom stall.

I threw my hands up in defeat.

"It's over!" I started to walk away feeling angry, hurt, and embarrassed. "I knew you were too good to be true! I shouldn't have ever married you. Whore!" I yelled.

I never wanted to believe the things I heard about the love of my life. I knew they were lies. There was no way she could do the things that she was accused of. I couldn't believe that she would lie and have multiple abortions. I grew angrier at myself for being fooled by her beauty. At that moment, I no longer felt bad for the things that I'd done. I caught up to my customer I was talking to and asked for a ride home.

CHAPTER 12

Suga

It was raining and foggy outside. I swerved as I tried to avoid an oncoming car. I called Marlon over twenty times and as expected, his voicemail continuously picked up. With tears clouding my vision, I frantically weaved in and out of the lanes. Horns blared as I carelessly forced cars out of my way. The only thing I thought about was getting home as quickly as possible. I had to save my marriage. As angry as Marlon was I knew he was at home putting all of my belongings on the front porch. The embarrassment would be too much for me to stand. The alcohol was subsiding, and snapping me out of my intoxication after what happened.

"Shit!" I yelled as I repeatedly hit the steering wheel.

What will our business partners think? What will I tell my friends and family?

I realized that I'd made the biggest mistake of my life.

SNOOK

Everything not only happened so fast, I didn't even remember how I got from the bar to the bathroom. It was all a blur. That was never the plan for our anniversary. It wasn't supposed to happen that way.

As I made the right-hand turn that led to our estate, I noticed a car sitting on the shoulder. If it were in front of one of the other homes down the road, I wouldn't have been suspicious. The car had tinted windows, which made it impossible to see the driver.

Oh my God! I thought.

Knots formed in my stomach as I pulled up to the house. It had been a while since I had a panic attack, but the suspicious sighting made me feel that one would come.

"Baby, where are you? I'm so sorry!" I yelled as I entered the front door.

I sat my handbag and keys down on the table. Marlon met me at the bottom of the stairs with my suitcase. Surprised to see him with my suitcase, I stumbled back from the side effects of the alcohol. He grabbed my arm to keep me from falling to the floor. I looked up at him to try to understand why he would help me after what I'd done to him. I noticed a smirk on his face, which made me nervous.

"Suga I know we need to talk, but not now. I'm too pissed off so right now you need to leave. You can't spend another night under this roof. I took care of you when you had nothing. I even paid for them fake ass breast you have," he said. He grabbed my chest.

I felt the dagger that was stabbed and twisted into my heart. Looking at the pain I caused on Marlon's face made my heart hurt. I wanted to say all of the things I regretted, but they were stuck inside of me. I wanted to confess all of the lies and all that I'd stolen from him. My mind raced. I couldn't catch my breath. Sweat formed all over my body as emptiness rose in the pit of my stomach. Darkness was the last thing I saw.

"Suga, baby, open your eyes," a voice spoke to me faintly.

I heard the voice of my mother speaking softly in the distance. The voice seemed far away. As I tried to reach for it, the voice faded back out again.

"Mom, I miss you. Where are you?" I yelled out.

I cried, yelled, and screamed, but there was no response. My body calmed as I drifted in and out. I could see myself in a kitchen. No kitchen I'd been in before. Walking into the living room, I saw my aunt and mother sitting and talking.

"Suga, baby, you need to wake up now," the voice said softly.

When I opened my eyes, I saw the most beautiful face. As tears ran down my face, I knew it was impossible because it was my mother, but it felt right. The last time I'd felt that way it was my Aunt Sable's voice that I heard.

"It's all right, baby. I'm here. Just sip a little water, while I get you something to put on your stomach," the voice said. I tried to clear my vision.

"Mom, is that you?" I tried to lift my head off of the pillow. A sharp pain struck me in the middle of my head, forcing me to lie back down. "Mom, come back. I need you! Please," I cried out.

SNOOK

The curtains in the room were opened with the sun shining down on me. Squinting from the sunlight, I tried to get a clear view of who was standing over me.

"Relax and lay still," the voice said softly.

I could hear the mystery person walk across the room as she closed the curtains. The room was quiet, still, and calm.

When I finally could open my eyes, I realized that the mystery woman was my mother. While she stood over me, I could feel her presence. Her recognizable voice gave me chills.

How could this be? I thought.

"You died years ago. I saw your dead body. I buried Teesa." Tears filled my eyes.

"It's me Suga. It's me. Please relax and just listen," she said, as she wiped my tears away. "I came as soon as Marlon and Redd called. I had to come and make sure you were okay," she said. She paced the floor, trying to find the words to explain. "I couldn't continue to stand by and watch you suffer because of this lie—"

"How could this be?" I interrupted. "I saw you. You were dead! I watched them bury you. Oh my God!" I yelled out.

I cried uncontrollably as the pain became relentless. I felt like I was trapped in a glass house. Silence surrounded us as we looked into each other's eyes. She was real and standing in front of me. Filled with confusion and many questions, the first thing I noticed was that she didn't have the mole above her lip. The voice was undeniably my mothers.

"Why didn't I recognize you after all these years? Why did you stay away?" I asked nervously.

"I'm so sorry for all the pain that I've caused you. I will never do anything to hurt you again, but there are some things that you have to know," she said. She continued to pace the floor. "You might not understand, but I had to run away. Your Aunt Sable was the one that died at our house that day. Do you remember her coming by the day before?" She grabbed a piece of tissue from the nightstand. "Your father was an evil son of a bitch and would've done anything in his power to make sure that I stayed true to him. As you know, I had a few flings here and there when he went jail, but that wasn't until after I found out about his wife."

I sat up in the bed as I tried to make sure I heard everything clearly, as thoughts randomly went through my mind. I tried to focus but was hypnotized by the sight of her.

"I stopped paying the lawyer and Linwood's commissary. I was hurt and finding out he was married was the last straw. I thought he would never get out, so I decided to live my life," she said. She sat on the foot of the bed. "A week before, he'd called and threatened me after I told him that I was done with him because of his possessive ways. I guess I struck a nerve. Do you remember anything?" she asked.

"No," I said. I wiped my tears with the back of my hand. "I blocked everything out. I didn't want to think about it. So, what happened to Aunt Sable?"

"When everything happened I panicked, and I fucked up!" she said, reliving that day. "I knew your father wanted to kill me after what I'd done to him so I took her bag and keys, and then I fled. I had to save you. You are more important to me than anything in this world," she said while holding my hand. "I couldn't let him hurt you. There was no telling what that man would've done if he knew someone had stolen two hundred thousand dollars from him. I had enough information to send a fine businessman like Linwood to prison for the rest of his life. I'm sure his wife had much more. I figured that was what a mistress was entitled to."

"What! You stole two hundred thousand dollars?" I asked as I fought to control the tone of my voice. "I didn't know that! Why didn't you tell me? We could've been together all these years. You just left! I cried for you every day after that. Why did you leave me?

I demanded and needed answers.

"You better snap out of that little girl shit and quick. Shit is real now. You're a grown ass woman. I did what I had to do for you, Suga. Do you think it was easy for me to stand by and watch you grow up from the sidelines? Hell no! That hurt me more than anything in this world. I knew that one wrong move could put both of our lives in jeopardy. When you become a mother, you'll understand my position. Right now, we are playing a dangerous game. Talking about it is dangerous. From here on out, I'm not your mother. Just call me auntie like you always have. We've just grown closer, like mother and daughter," she ordered.

I sat on the bed feeling like I was on a deserted island. I stared out of the window, thinking about how wrong life had gone. First, getting caught by my husband receiving oral sex in a filthy bathroom and secondly, waking up to my dead mother.

I must've been a bad person to deserve this, I thought.

We talked the entire night, catching up on the mother and daughter things that were missed over the years. My spirits were lifted from her presence. I knew that from here on out things would be different. My mother was back in my life and there was a possibility my husband may not be. Not knowing what to do about my marriage, I decided to give Marlon his space.

CHAPTER 13

Marlon

I sat at my desk unable to concentrate on the inventory sheets that I blankly stared over. Suga had been on my mind all day. As much as she hurt me, I missed her pretty smile, goofy laugh, and her sweet smell. She was missed when I got hungry. She catered to me, and that was what I missed the most. Although her behavior was scandalous, I undeniably loved her.

Business was better than ever. I ventured out and invested some of my profits into real estate, which proved to be a lucrative business decision. I had done it all for her. I wanted my wife and kids to live comfortably and enjoy the lifestyle I provided. I'd heard the phone ring consistently for twenty minutes.

"Damn it! Somebody answer the damn phone! What am I paying you for?" I yelled out of my office door.

We had clients that placed orders over the phone when they were unable to come into the store.

"Yes, Marlon. I mean Mr. Cole. We have special orders being called in for the new pendants that are coming in next week," Kendra said, as she sashayed across the office floor. "They've been taking calls all morning and working the floor. Everything is fine," she said.

"Make sure you transfer all of my personal calls to me. I have them routed to the store," I said, pushing around the paper on my desk. "I'm waiting on an important phone call."

I looked up to see Kendra staring down at me with her seductive smile. I knew her kind all too well and realized I was married to it. She was tempting, but I was not in the mood.

"Get the phones and keep my customers happy," I said. I shooed her out of my office.

Kendra noticed all the paperwork piled up on my desk.

"Well, you know I also have experience in bookkeeping as well," she said. Leaning over my desk, she wrapped my tie around her finger. "I think I might be able to help you out around here until Suga is better. I hate to see you like this; all wound up," she said with a pouty voice. "You have all the help you need right here. You just have to utilize it."

She let go of my tie and sat at Suga's desk.

Knowing she was just looking for a way to wiggle her way in I said, "I got this."

"This feels good," she said, rolling around in the leather office chair.

She placed her hands on the desk, pretending to handle business. I knew she was jealous of Suga and wished she were in her shoes.

SNOOK

"Kendra, you need to get out of my wife's chair and out of my office. Whatever you're thinking, you need to get it out of your head. I told you what happened between us was a one-time thing. You're supposed to be Suga's girl. How would this look?" I said, trying to remain quiet. "Our little secret is just that, our secret. We can't do this here. If you can't get with it, then you might have to find yourself another job." I walked her to the office door.

"Whatever! You just remember who is running this shit," she said. She pointed her finger in my face. "I know you don't want child support knocking at your door, now do you? Threaten me again about this bullshit ass job and you will see who will need a new job. You don't want your sweet little Suga to find out that her godchild is your biological daughter, do you?" She looked me up and down.

I gave her a cold stare. I knew she was looking for a reaction, but I wasn't going to give her the satisfaction.

"Mr. Cole, I'm going to help the customers now." Kendra sashayed out of the office.

I could've cared less about Kendra's threat. She wasn't crazy enough to let Suga know that we conceived a child together. Her threats always fell on deaf ears. As long as she received her commission checks every week, she had nothing to complain about. She had more to lose if she did tell. She was married with a child by her husband and according to the Commonwealth of Virginia her husband was the father.

I just wanted to keep her mouth shut. Offering her a job in exchange for her silence provided her more than fair child support disguised as commission checks. I didn't want to be a part of the baby's life. Dee was a great father, and it didn't make sense for the child to be confused. It was easy to do extra things for the child since she was Suga's goddaughter.

Although I hated to admit it, Kendra was right. Someone had to pick up the slack during Suga's absence and quick.

Maybe I should call and check on her, I thought.

I missed her so much. Just when I decided to follow my heart, I quickly remembered how easy it was for her to give it up at a club. Hurt and embarrassment overwhelmed me in a matter of minutes thinking about it. Although, there was a small crowd left in the club that night word quickly spread. All I wanted was to be out of the marriage and at the cheapest price possible. There were millions in cash and assets that were to be divided among us. The stores were tied into most of the assets, and I couldn't afford to lose my life's work. I was the one who sought out numerous investors for my business venture. The investor's returns were more than they anticipated. I cringed as I thought about what would ultimately happen if I divorced Suga. That was something that wasn't in our future plans. I thought I found my queen, and we were supposed to be together until the end. I was on the fence about the idea, but I needed to hear her voice.

CHAPTER 14

Teesa

Rushing through the door while dragging grocery bags, I hurried to the phone as it rang repeatedly. The dial tone blared in my ear as the caller hung up. I looked around the house and noticed how dark the living room was. I assumed that Suga must've been in the bed the entire day. Making my way into the kitchen, I sat the bags on the kitchen counter with oranges rolling onto the countertop. The phone rang again as Suga dragged her feet while entering into the kitchen.

"Girl, it's time for you to get yourself together. It's been three days, and you can use some fresh air," I said. I picked up the oranges and placed them into the bowl on the table. "Answer that phone!"

I pulled back the curtains to let in the sunlight. With her robe hanging from her body, Suga walked over to answer the phone.

"Hello?" she answered dryly.

I waited for her response as she stared into the receiver.

"Hello?" she said again with an attitude. "Whoever this is, you need to speak up before I hang up!" she yelled.

I snatched the phone from her, wanting to know who it was.

"Hello?" I said softly.

"Hi Aunt Sable, this is Marlon. Can I speak with Suga?"

"Sure Marlon, hold on," I replied as I handed the phone to Suga. I covered the phone and whispered, "Speak to him."

Suga snatched the phone from me while rolling her eyes.

"Hey," she said nonchalantly.

"Hey, how are you feeling?" Marlon asked.

"Hey, I'm fine now. How are you?" she asked with a smile on her face.

As tears ran down Suga's face, the sound of his voice must've filled her heart with love. She was hurting, and I knew he was too. I walked into the bedroom and picked up the other phone to listen in.

"I have a lot on my mind as you may know. I wanted to check up on you and make sure that you were doing better after you blacked out at the house. I called your Aunt Sable when it happened because I knew she would take care of you. I know there are some things that we need to discuss so I was wondering if you could come by the house so that we can sort things out," Marlon said.

Suga sat on the phone silently as Marlon rambled on about things that needed to be addressed between them. After hanging up, I tiptoed back into the kitchen to comfort her. Unaware that I'd eavesdropped on the call, Suga shared

SNOOK

that he wanted her to come over so that they could talk. Leery of the plans, I knew that she was an adult and had to deal with her problems. I now wondered if her pain was from my disappearance.

CHAPTER 15

Suga

I wanted to leap through the phone and into his arms while speaking to Marlon. When reality hit me, I knew it wouldn't be that easy.

How could I face him after my reckless behavior?

Later that day, I was nervous as I entered the driveway of our estate. I placed the car into park as I glanced behind me. It was a beautiful day, and I noticed that the hedges were trimmed at the entrance of the driveway. I slid down into the seat and let out a long sigh. I worried Marlon for weeks to have the landscaper trim the hedges at the entrance. They blocked my view when I pulled out into the street, and I worried I would hit someone.

"You should drive more carefully because nothing is wrong with the hedges. Look both ways before pulling out of the driveway," he'd say.

SNOOK

Lord, help me. Please don't let this man leave me, Lord. You know my heart and know that I love him. Please forgive me for all the wrong that I have done in this marriage. I couldn't stand to lose my husband.

It was then that I realized how much I would lose. The marriage wasn't perfect, but I did love him. I deeply regretted not having his child. I realized that would be the glue that would bond us forever. I looked up the driveway to our lifeless home.

A blaring horn behind me woke me from the private pity party in my head. In the rearview mirror, I noticed Marlon waiting for me to move. Initially, he appeared happy to see me, and within moments his expression changed.

I pulled the car closer to the house. My mind and heart raced at a hundred miles a minute. I pulled into my usual parking space but didn't quite feel like it was mine anymore. I dreaded the conversation that ultimately may be the ending of our marriage. Over the past few days, I tried to forget about what happened at the club. The pain of that night was like the day I thought my mother died. That was something I had to face head on. It was lights, camera, and action!

CHAPTER 16

Marlon

*I*t felt as though my heart would tear through my shirt as I pulled up and noticed Suga's car in the driveway. Exiting our vehicles, I wanted to hug, kiss, and tell her how much I loved her. It appeared she had the same urge, but neither of us acted on it. I unlocked the front door and held it open for her to enter. The elephant in the room followed us into the living room. The sun shined through the bay windows. I looked out remembering how Suga enjoyed sitting in the window while reading a book.

"Let's get to it. There isn't any need to prolong things," I said, snapping out of my daydream. "Suga, that shit you did at the club was foul. You hurt me, and now you've fucked up this marriage. I don't know if things can be repaired. How can I stay married to a bitch that got her pussy ate in a club bathroom?" I said angrily. "You did this!" I screamed as spit flew from my mouth like a pit bull.

SNOOK

Suga sat quietly. I'd never spoke to her in that manner. The word *bitch* tore through me like a rocket, so I knew it hurt her. Unfortunately, I couldn't avoid the love I felt for her.

"All that shit you've done, like killing my babies, is fucked up!" I said angrily.

Searching for a sign of remorse, I looked at her suspiciously.

"I'm so sorry. I don't know why I chose to have the abortions. I was scared," she sobbed. "As for what happened at the club, it was as if I had no control of myself. My mind was screaming *no*, but I couldn't stop it. I tried."

I knew Suga was clever when it came to coming up with a lie. I wasn't buying it. There was no way she was going to walk out with everything I'd built.

"I think somebody slipped me something," she blurted out. "Yeah, that had to be it. I'll never do anything like that again," she said convincingly.

Tears filled my eyes, but my pride took over.

"Look, you can have the house for now. I will get an apartment until we can get things sorted out. We have a business to run, and that's our livelihood," I said coldly.

"All right, but I want you to take some time and think about this. Please, don't make any drastic decisions about divorce. Promise me that we will try to work things out. I love you. I need you, Marlon," she pleaded. "You're all that I have in this world."

"Suga, you know I love you. You are the only woman I've ever loved. I just don't know if I can handle this. You've fucked up! I was the only man you've been with, and now some random fucker has had my wife," I said, as the anger quickly reappeared. "I have to go before I do something I'll regret."

Since she'd never seen me so angry, she knew the only thing left to do was for me to leave. Although I didn't want to leave my home, I knew it was for the best.

CHAPTER 17

Suga

I sat alone in our big empty home. The love we'd shared and experienced made me feel regret. Tears flowed down my face from the heaviness of the pain I'd caused. I cried for the babies that I denied life, which caused Marlon to miss out on fatherhood. I thought about all the selfish things I'd done in my life.

Why didn't I have his babies? Oh, it was because I'm a selfish bitch! I thought.

I wandered through the house and imagined our kids running and playing. The image of Marlon enjoying fatherhood, and appreciating me for bringing his children into the world was gratifying. In the kitchen, I saw myself cooking dinner and smiling proudly at my family. Reality hit home quick when my cell phone broke my thoughts.

"Hello?" I said when I answered the phone.

"Hey. Where have you been?" Kendra asked.

"Hey. I'm just going through some things. It's nothing I can't handle," I said, trying to keep her under the radar. "How's Destiny?" I asked, trying to change the subject.

"She's fine with her bad self. You've got to see her. She's getting so big. I miss you Suga. When are you coming back to work?" she asked.

I knew she could care less when I returned to work. She wanted as much time alone with Marlon as possible.

"I'm just taking some time off. I'll call you back a little later. Love you," I said. My stomach turned from the sound of her voice.

"Love you too. If you need to talk, I'm here. Talk to you later," Kendra said before hanging up.

CHAPTER 18

Teesa

I sat in my room thinking about Suga. She hadn't called after meeting with Marlon. I worried about her and figured she'd tell me what was discussed when she was ready. However, I felt the need to call and check on her.

"Hey, Suga. How did things go?" I asked curiously.

"Hey Auntie, I'm fine. I'm at home now so I won't be back tonight," she said in a strange tone.

I didn't mind her calling me Auntie because that was what I told her to do. By her tone, I figured someone was there with her.

"That's fine. I hope you're at home working things out with your husband. You've been away long enough," I said, giving a slight chuckle.

"Yes, I am. Everything is cool now so don't worry about me. I know he loves me, and I love him. That's all that matters. Thank you for taking care of me the last couple of days. I don't know what I would've done without you," she said gratefully.

"Girl, it's nothing. That's what family is for. You should go see a doctor about those fainting spells. The last time you had one was at your graduation party. Was that the first time?" I asked. "I don't recall you having fainting spells when you were younger," I added.

Confusing my role with Suga, I had to return to pretending to be her aunt.

"You know things were perfect before your death. We lived well and wanted for nothing," she whispered while taking me down memory lane. "I loved my father and for your information my first fainting spell happened after finding your dead body!" she added angrily. "So, keep pretending to be somebody you're not. I don't need you now, *Sable!*" she said before slamming down the phone.

The initial shock overpowered the hurt, but I deserved it. I abandoned and left Suga to grow up without a mother. I wasn't there to show her how to be a lady and teach her life's lessons. She was out there in the world trying to figure it out on her own. At the time, it was easier to leave things the way they were. I pretended that *Teesa* died and no matter what I said or did, I knew my decision was best for the both of us.

CHAPTER 19

Suga

I wanted to be with my husband, but it was clear that it would take some time and effort to get back into his good graces. I had so much to tell him. I wanted to share the truth about Teesa, and the money she'd stolen from Linwood. Most of all, I wanted him to know that I was ready to be a mother. The mother of his children. It was time to be the woman that Marlon needed. After realizing that there was a chance that I'd lose him, I was more determined than ever to keep my man and the money at all cost.

Turning off my cell phone was the only way I could avoid an argument with my mother. There was enough going on in my life, and I had to deal with each issue separately. I wanted her to hurt for all the years I mourned. Reliving the day I found her dead body traumatized me for years. That began my downward spiral that eventually caused my fainting spells. The pain I carried around quickly turned into anger towards her.

Who in the hell does she think she is? Does she think she can come back into my life after all of these years? How can I accept her as my mother after all of the pain she has caused me? Hell no! Fuck her! She fucked up my life. I don't owe her shit! Why come back into my life now? I thought.

I was exhausted from the events the last few days. I felt the weight of the stress. I headed to the master bathroom for some much needed meditation. As I walked into the bedroom, I noticed it was exactly the way I'd left it. The red dress I'd decided not to wear still lay at the foot of the bed. The matching pumps sat on the floor. I walked over and picked up the dress.

"He is just too good to me," I said.

I held the dress against my body and admired it in the mirror.

The bed was untouched, which meant Marlon hadn't slept in it. I walked into my closet to hang up the dress and examined the rewards from the lavish lifestyle he provided. There were designer clothes, bags, jewelry, and shoes that made the closet look like a small boutique. When depressed I'd pull out all of my things and admire them one by one. Material things made me feel good. Not having a mother, father, sister, brother, or children made me feel vulnerable. That mindset made me desire the need to cover myself with beautiful things.

As I glanced around the room, admiring the fine décor, I noticed a wrapped gift. With a red bow tied around it, my eyes gleamed as it sat on my dresser waiting to be opened. It was normal for Marlon to shower me with gifts and written poems. I loved the way he made me feel. I wondered if he did those things because he felt sorry for me. I walked away leaving the box on the dresser untouched.

This must've been an anniversary gift from Marlon. I don't deserve it.

Entering the master bathroom, I turned on the water in the Jacuzzi tub. I added some lavender aromatherapy oil and lit some Yankee candles. I took deep breaths as the steam and lavender drifted into the air. The curiosity of what Marlon bought ate away at me. I slowly undressed, taking quick glances into the mirror. I imagined one of the many times Marlon pretended he wasn't watching me undress in the bathroom. I'd seduce him by entertaining his thoughts of pleasure. I looked into the bedroom, which gave me an instant reminder that he wasn't secretly watching me.

As I stepped one foot into the tub, the curiosity of the gift got the best of me. I quickly stepped back out and grabbed my robe off of the hook. As my wet footprints soaked the carpet, I ran into the bedroom and picked up the box. I opened the card taped under the red bow.

I will always love, honor, and cherish you as my wife. Here is something that took time, patience, and effort just like this marriage.

Happy Anniversary Suga baby!
Love Always,
Marlon

I removed the wrapping paper and opened the box. There was a Hermès Birkin handbag sitting inside. I couldn't believe it. I held the soft leather bag close to my body, inhaling the strong leather scent. I fell back on the bed while holding it close as if it were Marlon hugging me.

"Oh my God, how did he know?" I said out loud.

This was one hell of a surprise. My nipples became erect as blood rushed to my center. When my private ritual was over, I soaked in the tub while releasing the stress of what would soon be my past. That was one hell of a surprise.

CHAPTER 20

Teesa

I couldn't believe the way Suga spoke to me. I wondered where it all had come from so suddenly. Her quick acceptance to finding out I was her mother must've finally ended. Suga's words hurt, and came through the phone line like a dagger in my heart. She had marital problems, but I never thought she'd shut me out. Every night I prayed for forgiveness.

I had business to handle before going back home. I figured the longer I stayed in the city, the more I put Suga's life in danger. There were three hundred thousand dollars in a bank deposit box with her name on it. Providing for her over the years, I'd spent all of the money I'd stolen from Linwood. I needed more to continue to live as Sable.

Linwood knew the government was onto him. He made arrangements to ensure his legal fees and family was provided for. His wife got the house, cars, and access to the personal and business bank accounts. I had the cash needed to pay off a few good men, which was set up to buy Linwood a reduced sentence. It assured he'd be released in two years or less. Instead, I made sure he received a lengthy sentence for making me his mistress.

Making the choice to come back into Suga's life as myself was tough. The love for my daughter was the reason behind making those choices. I fought for her forgiveness and trust.

I stared at my phone fighting the temptation to call Suga and apologize, but instead I cried. I cried for Sable, Suga, and myself. Tears welled up in my eyes and fell heavily. With each tear, I released years of hiding, lying, deception, and loneliness.

After all of these years, why should she forgive me? Besides, I abandoned her when she needed me the most, I thought.

There were things Suga didn't understand, and wouldn't until she'd become a mother. Mothers must make tough decisions, and not all of them will please others. I did what I believed I had to do to save her. When the time was right, we would be together again. Until then as my mother use to say, "*The truth shall set you free.*" Unfortunately, the truth would land me in prison for the rest of my life or worse.

CHAPTER 21

Marlon

I returned to my riverfront loft in the city, my sanctuary. It was my place of residence for the past few days. Suga didn't know that I'd never terminated the lease. I was sure that she expected me to let it go when we were married. I didn't want to be reminded of her, and staying in our house would've driven me insane. Besides the house and everything in it, I did for her. There were many reminders of the mistakes that I'd made, and the main one was Suga.

No longer able to hold back the tears, they poured down my face like a waterfall. I glanced at her photo that hung on the wall. I loved Suga and couldn't deny it, but she was dead weight to me at that moment. The more that was revealed about her the worse I felt. Finding out she had the abortions was the worst of them all. I should've confronted her after Kendra told me. Knowing her envious feelings toward Suga.

Initially, I didn't believe her. A part of me believed that she wouldn't do those things.

The thoughts of betrayal made me regret going to such lengths to make sure I provided everything she desired. I allowed her to come into my life as a queen and sit on the throne. I never gave her a reason not to trust me. I relished in the trust that she had for me and felt guilty about it. Betraying her trust by sleeping with her best friend and fathering a child with Kendra was a crime against the heart. Fathering the child was not just a crime, but punishable by death in Suga's eyes.

After that conversation with Suga, I was forced to consider saving our marriage. She was still my wife, and I've loved her since the first time I'd laid eyes on her. Her innocence accompanied with everything else just seemed right. Finding out over time that she was damaged made me want to provide and protect her. The beautiful outer shell covered up all of the shattered pieces left inside of her. After learning of her issues that stemmed from her parents absence, I thought that I could fix it for her. So, making her happy became the most important thing to me.

A happy wife, happy life, I thought.

After the money and gifts, I then realized that only God could help her. Suddenly, my cell phone vibrated and I noticed it was a text from Suga.

Thanks for the gift, baby. It was just what I wanted, but I want you more. I love and miss you. Please come back home.

After reading the text several times, I felt an array of emotions. I wanted to go back home and work through our issues, but a part of me wished I'd never met her. Knowing she had my heart in the palm of her hands caused me to melt away. Tears fell down my face as I recounted the image of my wife and another man. It hurt like hell as my anger intensified. I picked up the remote from the coffee table and threw it at the television. I missed it by inches as I watched the remote slam into the wall. I kicked over the glass cocktail table and watched all of its contents fall to the floor. I burned with fire. With every thought of wanting to be with her, the angrier I became.

How could we go back to being a happy couple when she was with another man? I thought.

It seemed easier to walk away and forget about her, but my heart was in a tug of war. After several minutes, I finally calmed down. Looking around at the demolished room, I noticed how I managed to tear everything off of the walls and turn over any and everything that wasn't bolted to the floor. Nothing in the room mattered to me but Suga.

I sobbed because I didn't know what to do to fix the damage. My tears were from karma's rage. I knew it was payback for committing the worst sin against my wife and living a lie. I was at the point of no return, which meant someone had to pay. I regretted letting that man walk out of the bathroom that night. I wished I choked Suga, and left her within inches of her life. I imagined bringing her back to life again, proving that I had the upper hand.

CHAPTER 22

Suga

I appreciated the time Marlon and I had a part. It gave me an opportunity to think about the night of our anniversary. I sat and wondered how I ended up with my thong around my ankles.

After spending thirty minutes looking at the text message, I decided to send it to Marlon. I put on one of his oversized white T-shirts, which made me feel close to him. Anticipating a return text or call, I pinned up my hair and executed my nightly beauty routine. After several minutes and periodic glances at my cell phone, I thought I may have missed his response.

I crawled into the California king sized bed and pulled up the covers. The smell of Marlon's scent woke up the senses between my thighs. What I would've given to have him between my legs at that moment. Working out our issues was necessary, but I knew sex wouldn't solve them.

SNOOK

With my cell phone in hand, I checked every minute to make sure I didn't miss his response. After an hour, Marlon still hadn't responded.

I should've heard something from him by now, I thought to myself.

He didn't check on me to make sure the house was locked, and the alarm was set. That was something he'd do every night before bed.

Maybe I should resend the text. Sometimes text messages don't go through the first time, especially with these new Smartphones, I thought.

After several minutes of back and forth conversations with myself, I decided not to resend it.

Times like this, Kendra's friendship was needed. She was once my ear and shoulder to cry on. Our relationship changed when I married Marlon. She didn't support my marriage like I supported hers. If it weren't for her Marlon, and I wouldn't have met. I was happy for her when she found love and started a family.

During our last conversation, Kendra fished for information. Instead of checking on me without ill intent, she wanted to know when I was returning to work. I wanted to call and tell her everything. Knowing what that outcome would be led me to lay in bed alone. The suspicious strain on our friendship helped me decide that a phone call to Kendra was out of the question.

Glancing at my phone again, I turned on the television for some form of distraction. I typed *I love you* into my phone and sent it to Marlon. Wanting him to know that I cared, I no longer allowed the thoughts of how worrisome I appeared. Tears filled my eyes with the idea of losing him. I once thought that Marlon would never leave me, but I was wrong.

As I dozed off, my cell phone rang,

"Hello?" I said with a groggy tone.

"Hey sweetness, can you talk?" the voice asked.

"It's late. Why are you calling me? I don't have anything to say to you. I could kill your ass for that shit you pulled the other night! What if Marlon was here?" I yelled into the phone.

"I knew he wasn't there. I saw how hurt he was when he left the club that night," the caller said while laughing. "What do you have on?"

"You're terrible. How can you be worried about what I have on at a time like this? I could lose everything messing around with you. Look, I don't think we should be speaking right now. I need to deal with my home life right now. That shit you pulled was fucked up. I don't try to come between you and your girl."

"Look, I understand you have a husband, but don't push me away. I've been there for you since day one. Even after you married his ass, I continued to stick around. I know that I can't be the man you need me to be, but I will do my best. I want you to know that I love you even if you choose him instead of me."

"Whatever bitch! As I said, that shit was fucked up, and you shouldn't have done that. What if he would've killed both of our asses in that bathroom? He doesn't even know you're a female or at least I don't think he noticed. He kept calling you a man," I replied.

"I'm sorry. We both were drunk, and things got out of hand. I hope you get your shit together. I want you to be happy. I'm out. My girl just pulled up."

"Fuck you and lose my number bitch! I swear to God, if you've fucked this up for me, I will kill you and that bitch!" I said before hanging up the phone.

I was wide awake and mad as hell. It was because of L.C. that I was in hot water with Marlon in the first place. L.C. lived next door to Uncle Redd so we'd known one another since we were kids. She was older, so I looked up to her like a big sister. As I came out of my shell and opened up, she became a true friend. I believed that I could talk to her about anything. We'd shared our secrets and inner feelings with one another.

Neither one of us were interested in boys at the time for our own reasons. Afraid of trusting anyone, I kept my distance. Relationships were something I wasn't ready for and as for L.C., she didn't quite have an interest in boys.

One day while listening to music at L.C.'s house, she made sure I was comfortable. Being guarded, it took months for me to relax around her. She sat beside me on the bed and laid her head on my shoulder. Pretending to be interested in the magazine, L.C. looked at me seductively.

"How come you don't have a man, Suga?" she asked.

"Why don't you have a boyfriend? Neither one of us is in a relationship right now," I said. We both laughed.

"Well, I know why I don't have a man. I'm not interested in guys like that. If I told you something, would you still be my friend? I don't want you to judge me the way everyone else does. It would hurt me to lose a good friend like you," she said, as she rubbed her fingers through my hair. "You know I would never jeopardize our friendship."

I was curious, so I sat up in the bed.

"What's wrong? I would never judge you. You didn't judge me," I said sincerely. "I value our friendship. Girl, I've shared everything with you and not once have you made me feel uncomfortable," I said. "Did you have your heart broken by one of these man whores out here or something?" I asked jokingly.

"Hell yeah! Who hasn't had their heart broken? That's not the reason. I'm attracted to women. I think I'm gay," she said reluctantly.

Shocked to hear her admit that she was gay, I thought maybe she was confused. I took a moment to take in what she'd shared.

"Are you sure you mean gay as in being exclusively with girls?" I asked.

"Yes Suga, I like girls! There I said it. It's so liberating," she said with a smile on her face.

"Wow, that's cool. I guess. It doesn't matter to me as long as it makes you happy."

As long as that girl isn't me, I thought to myself.

Still grinning, L.C. showed her perfectly straight white teeth. She reached out to hug me. As I welcomed the hug, I hoped it would end the awkward conversation. While sharing an embrace, L.C. leaned in to kiss me. In shock, I couldn't move. We looked at one another as we tried to read one another's reaction. Quickly pulling away, I looked at her strangely.

SNOOK

"I'm surprised you didn't give me a bloody lip," she said jokingly.

I didn't know what to do. L.C.'s bold move had me stumped. It was strange but felt good. As curiosity took over my mind and body, I closed my eyes and anticipated another kiss. I knew she'd be bold enough to try it again, but that time I'd hoped she would.

While caressing and running her fingers through my long black hair, she forced me to tilt my head back. With my neck exposed, she held me close and kissed my neck leading from my chin to my collarbone. Sending shock waves through my body, I quietly moaned. The feeling of ecstasy made my body tingle all over. The muscles between my legs contracted, which sent warm sensations to the pit of my stomach. I throbbed for her, and she knew my body signals gave her the green light. She laid me back on the bed and slowly removed my clothes. She repeatedly introduced me to seduction and ecstasy. As the silence lingered in the room, I shed tears of pleasure and appreciation. My friend had introduced me to my new best friend, an orgasm.

CHAPTER 23

Marlon

After hours of sulking, I found myself on the road heading home. Scattered thoughts in my mind led me to be with Suga. Finding out who she was with that night at the club was the only way to eliminate the x-factor. There was no way I could move forward without that issue being resolved. In those cases, I knew just who to turn to, and that was Dee.

"What it do?" Dee said after answering the phone on the first ring.

"Man, shit. I need to holla at you about something," I said.

"I knew you would call your boy. I was giving you time to clear your head on this one. I know you, man. I'm glad you called. I have some information if you need it. You have to prepare yourself for this one. Matter of fact, I know you're not ready for this shit."

"That's why I need you to come through tomorrow. Suga got me fucked up, Dee! I got too much to lose and she got me twisted," I said.

Dee sat silently on the phone as I rambled on and on about Suga hurting me. He admitted to knowing about the incident at the club and didn't hesitate in sharing that he knew the identity of the individual. He warned me that the information would blow my mind.

"You know that I love you and Suga. You got this," he added.

"Come through," I said.

"Okay, I got your back," he said before hanging up.

The stress gradually faded after discussing my problems with Dee. I thought about our marriage vows. The day I married Suga, I meant every word and still did. She was mine, and I wouldn't let anyone change that.

Knowing that Dee had my back, I knew he kept his ear to the pavement. He didn't have a problem getting information and I couldn't shake the fact that Dee gave me a subtle warning about who it was.

Was it someone that I knew?

I was so shocked by what I saw, that I didn't get a good look at the guy. There was something strange, but I couldn't put my finger on it.

After pulling into the driveway, I came to the conclusion that I couldn't spend another night away from her. I felt like a bitch running home. I sat in my truck looking at the house wondering if she was inside thinking of me. I took a deep breath and released my apprehensions about going home to her.

CHAPTER 24

Suga

The blaring sounds of the alarm clock on the nightstand startled me. The sun beamed through the bedroom window as I rolled over to hit the snooze button. Squinting to see the time on the clock, it read seven o'clock. It was time for my morning jog before starting the day. After several minutes of contemplating, I decided to remain in the bed.

A sound came from down the hall. I jumped up. With my heart racing, I tried to concentrate on the sound. When there was a moment of silence, I second guessed myself. I wondered if I'd heard anything at all. The sound of the guest bedroom door opening squeaked throughout the house. As I tiptoed out of the door, I peeked down the hallway. The green light blinked on the alarm panel, which hung on the wall outside of the guest bedroom door. Realizing I didn't set the alarm the night before, I panicked and rushed to the phone. As I picked it up to dial 9-1-1, I heard a voice.

"Good morning," Marlon said, standing in the bedroom doorway.

Frightened by his sudden appearance, I jumped and watched as the phone dropped to the floor.

"I'm sorry. I didn't mean to scare you," he said regretfully. I was relieved it was him and silently thanked God. "I'm sorry I should've let you know I was here. Hang up the phone before the police show up at my front door."

He entered the room, remaining clear of the bed. A week ago, sex would've easily ended our fight. I noticed he stayed out of striking distance. Still shaken, I picked up the phone and sat it back into the cradle on the nightstand.

"I missed you, baby. When did you come home?" I asked.

The air was thick between us, and there was no denying it. I chose my words wisely and was careful not to upset him.

"I came in late last night. I know you don't like to be alone."

Walking over to my side of the bed, he reached for my hand. My body shook from his touch. His expression allowed me to see the fight in his eyes. His nostrils flared as he fumed with anger. Trying to remain calm, I watched him take in deep breaths.

"Honey, why don't I make us some breakfast," I said, sliding my hand from his grip.

"No. You need to tell me what happened that night," Marlon said.

"I know…I want to be honest with you about everything, but I'm afraid. I don't want you to look at me differently."

I was ready and willing to lay it all on the line. I dropped to my knees sobbing, but Marlon wasn't moved by my performance. Looking at me with pity, he watched as I cried a river.

"You should be on your knees begging," he said. He reached for my face. "Tell me what the hell is going on."

Helping me to my feet, we sat down on the bed. I shook uncontrollably as Marlon tried to keep me calm. Assuring an attack didn't happen, he reached into the nightstand and grabbed my medicine. He handed me the bottle while remaining focused on the issues at hand.

"No. I have to do this with a clear head. I'll be okay," I said, sobbing.

"Are you sure? I don't want you to pass out on me." He put the medicine back into the nightstand. "I want to know what my wife is out there doing. If I wanted a whore, I would've stayed in the streets."

"Don't pretend that you're perfect because you're not. Do you think I believe I've been the only woman you've fucked since we've been together? I don't think so. You just haven't been caught," I said defensively.

"This is not about me. This is about you getting caught getting your pussy ate out on our anniversary!"

Watching our world fall apart right before us, we stared at each other as tears fell down our faces.

"Suga, I love you. I knew this shit wasn't going to be easy. Just tell me who he is," he pleaded.

"First of all, there isn't another man," I said, hoping it would hurt him less. "She was a childhood friend who lived next door to Uncle Redd."

Confused, Marlon stood up as he began pacing the floor. He looked at me as if he didn't comprehend what I said. Instantly, it seemed like a light bulb went off.

"Oh shit! That was a bitch?" he said, laughing. "You like bitches? Damn, you should've told me that a long time ago. I had a few chicks that wouldn't have mind coming home with us."

Marlon continued to pace the floor as he pounded his fist into his hands. Nerves fluttered inside of me as I prayed he wouldn't hit me. I hoped the news would be less insulting since it was a woman.

"Baby, just hear me out. It's not what you think. Please, calm down and listen to me," I pleaded as I cautiously walked towards him.

"You're right, that's why I'm here. I had to know the truth," he said.

Marlon sat down and looked around the room in disbelief. Listening to my confession was more than he'd expected.

"I felt sorry for you. I was empathetic to everything that you've been through. I had no idea how fucked up you are!" he yelled as reality sat in.

"First of all, I was drunk as hell," I said. "You know how much I had to drink. I was upset with you after I watched you dance with that woman."

Blaming it on the alcohol was the only excuse for my impulsive behavior. I was relieved after admitting the truth about L.C. I had no idea where our marriage stood, but I knew that it was important that I told him the truth. Being smart, I kept the hidden fact that I had an ongoing relationship with L.C. when I had the taste for it. I wanted to be honest, not stupid. The odds were against me, but I had to take a chance.

CHAPTER 25

Marlon

After listening to Suga's confession, I knew there were decisions I had to make. Deep in my heart, the marriage was over. Even if I hadn't found out that she was an undercover lesbian, she would've eventually found out that I had a child with her best friend. I knew I couldn't hide that forever.

I sat on the edge of the bed watching her undress in the bathroom. She was beautiful, and her body was perfect. Knowing I had to let her go gave me mixed emotions about anyone else having her. I despised the hold she had on me.

I watched as she walked towards me and kissed me gently on my forehead. I was sure she was anticipating rejection, but I couldn't. She slowly moved down to my lips, while using her tongue to part my reluctant lips. We shared a passionate kiss, and there was no doubt the kiss fueled my anger. In my body, the pain and desire mingled.

CHAPTER 26

Teesa

Using my cell phone's GPS, I searched for Cole's Jewelry Store. I wanted to speak with Marlon in hopes he'd convince Suga to accept my calls. I got her voicemail with every attempt. With so much left to discuss, I regretted not telling her the entire truth about the night of Sable's death. In the time of panic, I realized that I didn't handle things properly. Because of Suga's fragile state, I became more worried. I hoped she didn't tell anyone about my true identity.

Listening to the voice from the GPS directing me to the store, I reached into my purse to make sure that I had my gun. I didn't go anywhere without it. Since I was living on the run, I never knew who'd recognize me when I came to visit.

I pulled up in front of the store and looked around the parking lot. It was almost noon, and the parking lot was full.

SNOOK

Pulling my dark sunglasses above my eyes, I walked into the store and instantly scanned the scene. I looked around, admiring the layout and design of the store.

You wouldn't know from the outside that it was decorated so beautifully, I thought.

As I scanned the crowd, I slid my glasses back on. I noticed the men in business suits and white T-shirts lined up at the jewelry cases. The women who accompanied the men picked out jewelry at the men's expense. As I browsed the cases, admiring the beautiful jewelry, I was approached by one of the employees.

"Welcome to Cole's Jewelry Store. Is there something I can help you with?" the young lady asked with a smile.

"Yes, I'm here to see Marlon Cole, please," I said in my business voice.

Unsure if she'd openly lead me to him, I wanted her to assume I was there on business.

"Yes, he is in his office. Please, follow me. I love your glasses. Umm…I'm sorry I didn't get your name," the young lady said.

"I didn't give it, but it's Sable," I said, as I frowned at the naïve sales woman.

Following her down the lavish hallway to Marlon's office, I observed the expensive artwork and tall unique floor vases that lined the walls. Money was definitely within my reach, and there was still one piece to the puzzle that I hadn't figured out.

"I think I have it from here," I said, as we approached the only door at the end of the hallway.

I looked up and noticed the gold name plate that read *Marlon and Suga Cole*.

"Let me know if I can assist you with anything else," she said, as she headed back to the front of the store.

The office door was closed, which prevented me from entering before knocking. Unable to see inside of the office, I removed my hat and shades. Then I placed them in my bag. I straightened my hair as I proceeded to knock as I opened the door. Startled by the sound of angry voices, I stopped in my tracks. Not wanting to interrupt, I stood still. I turned to walk away when the voices became louder and more distinguishable. I recognized Marlon's voice. The woman's voice was not quickly identified. I assumed it was an unhappy customer or employee. While I waited, I discreetly listened in on the heated conversation.

"Look, maybe this arrangement is not going to work. I only did this to keep the peace, but this shit isn't working," Marlon said.

"Now you want to do the right thing? This was your idea, not mine," the female voice said angrily.

"Look, Kendra, I didn't know you were going to act crazy and shit. We both knew what we did was a mistake, but now there is an innocent child involved. I don't love you, nor am I going to leave my wife for your ass. Do you understand?" Marlon asked.

Knowing who the female voice belonged to, I wanted to hear more of what was transpiring between Marlon and Suga's best friend.

"I sure do. You don't want your precious Suga to know

that I gave you something she never would. I don't want you and never did. I just hate to see my friend with a low life like you. You're right this shit isn't working. All those checks you cut every week, well you better figure out another way to get them to me. I better have every red cent, or there will be consequences," Kendra said.

"Bitch, I don't have to do shit! That's your husband's job. He's the father or did you forget who signed the birth certificate? I did this because it was the right thing to do for my daughter. Now get your ass out of my store and don't come back in here. I love my wife, and it's time that you realized that. This shit here is over!" Marlon yelled.

Even more shocked by what I heard, I was furious knowing that the man my daughter married was a cheating ass bastard. He was supposed to love, honor and cherish her. I stood in silence, listening to his painful confession. I wanted to call Suga and tell her about her husband's indiscretions, but I had to be smart. It was not the time to go to her with that information. I knew I was on her shit list, and figured she may not believe me. I had to create a plan to earn her trust back.

"No matter how you decide to sneak money my way, it better get to me. She is your daughter no matter whose name is on her birth certificate. I love Suga as well, and I wish to spare her all the graphic details of our history. Sooner or later she will find out. She is my best friend, and we will always be there for one another. She's a smart girl, and when she figures this out, I won't deny it," Kendra said.

"We both know that Suga isn't to be fucked with, and

you're also a smart girl. Now I have a business to run," Marlon said.

Assuming Kendra would be walking out of the office any minute, I rushed away from the door. Startled by my presence, Kendra jumped when she saw me standing in the hallway. Apparently upset from their fueled conversation, she hurried down the hall. Kendra wiped her tears as she approached the end of the hall as she looked back at me strangely. We stared each other down with no words exchanged.

I walked into the office to find an upset Marlon behind his desk.

"Hey, Sable. What's up? What are you doing here?" he asked, quickly putting on a smile.

He stood up to greet me. While we embraced, Marlon quickly pulled back at my aloof response.

"Hi Marlon, nice place you have here," I said, taking a seat in a nearby chair.

"Thanks. I'm glad you could see it. Is there something I can get for you?" he asked nervously.

"I'm not here for pleasure. I came to talk to you about Suga. I wanted to check on her, but she hasn't returned any of my calls," I said, looking around the office suspiciously.

"We're doing fine now. We talked, and everything is okay. I don't know why she hasn't returned your phone calls," he said.

"Are you sure everything is okay? From what I could hear, it seems you both have some unfinished business," I said, choosing my words carefully.

"Why do you think that?" Marlon said. He cleared his throat.

I watched as he shifted in his leather office chair.

"I heard your conversation with Miss Kendra. How could you do that to Suga?"

"Look, you don't know what you're talking about. This is between me and my wife," he said defensively.

Instead of him admitting his faults and asking for advice, he became defensive. The pride he expressed I knew all too well.

"I know that you love her, but you have to fix this. The worst thing you could do to your wife is to commit adultery, but you've brought a child into the picture. Marlon, for a woman, that's another type of pain. Hell, you don't have kids with your wife! What do you think this would do to her?" I paused. "You know how fragile she is."

I watched as stress and anxiety came over him. He put his face in his hands, covering up the shame he'd hidden.

"You have to fix this fast. I came here to talk to you about something important, but from the sound of things you have no clue to what's going on. Since Suga hasn't trusted you enough to tell you, then why should I?" I asked.

"What are you talking about? Suga told me about her past with her girlfriend. I told you we've spoken about everything!"

Surprised at his last statement, I completely gave him a pass on the way he raised his voice. I knew Suga was spoiled and sheltered, but I had no idea about a lesbian relationship. I made a mental note that that was another thing I failed at when it came to her. Time was of the essence, and the longer I hung around town trying to reach out to her, the closer I came to being discovered. I was more concerned with my daughter's well-being than my own.

"There's something that I need to talk to Suga about and soon. We had a disagreement, and I need to smooth things over with her before I leave."

"Why don't you come by the house tonight? I'm sure she'll be there. I have some business to take care of, and I'll be running late getting home. That should give you some time alone with her. I know that she loves you so things will be okay between you two," he said reassuringly.

"Thanks, I'll make sure I stop by later. I just wanted you to know that I've always loved you and trusted that you'd take care of her. Make sure that you tell your wife what's going on before it's too late. Nothing good comes out of this type of situation, and I fear that someone is going to get hurt," I said with concern.

"Look, I told you've I got this," he said.

CHAPTER 27

Dee

*m*an, you can't keep wearing me out like this," I said as I rolled over and smacked her on the ass.

Suga and I had been having weekly rendezvous for months. I walked over to the thermostat to adjust the temperature. Sweat dripped down my naked body as Suga lay across the bed. I admired her silhouette from under the sheets.

I don't know how she handles all this dick, I thought.

"You can't keep wearing *me* out like that," she replied while panting heavily. "I don't know about you, but who cares if they find out after what they've done to us. Karma is a bitch, and it's a fucked up situation," Suga said with bitterness in her voice.

"Yeah it is, but we both love them and still want our relationships," I said while wiping Suga's juices from my body. "In the beginning, this shit was like a pain pill for me.

It helped me feel better, so I guess it is fucked up. What they don't know can't hurt them," I replied.

"I agree with the fact that it makes you feel better. After you had told me about the blood test, you found, I blamed myself. I had no one else to turn to but you. I wished he'd been man enough to tell me," she said regretfully.

"That bitch has always wanted what you had. She envied you. It was a love-hate relationship. Just knowing that it was a one-time thing that resulted in a child was enough for me," I said. I sat on the edge of the bed. "Marlon doesn't give a fuck about Kendra. He has only loved you. I can't blame him for keeping it from you. I wouldn't want to lose you either. I love Kendra and my daughter, but I don't like Kendra's ways."

I knew what we were doing was wrong, but today was different. Initially, it began with Suga confiding in me during our phone conversations. With the both of us in pain, she was vulnerable and instead of dealing with the issue, I convinced her to get even. It didn't seem like such a bad idea, but no matter how often we slept together it didn't change anything. It was time to deal with the situation, and although I enjoyed fucking the shit out of Suga's fine ass, the secret betrayal was getting old.

"Suga, I think that this has gone on long enough. Don't get me wrong, it was damn good. I just think we should confront them so that we can move on."

"I love Marlon and I do want to work things out with him even though they've kept this shit from us," she said, as she put on her clothes.

"I know, lately I've been thinking the same thing. This is

not what we want. We're doing this for the wrong reasons, and the hurt they've caused is going to increase if we don't address it. I love Marlon like a brother, and I know that what happened between him and Kendra was a mistake. I forgave him a long time ago. As for Kendra, I've never trusted her ass," I said slyly.

"Now, that's a typical man speaking. Why is it so easy for you to forgive your boy, but punish the female?" Suga asked, looking at me strangely.

"That's just how it is. It's like a code men have." I shrugged my shoulders.

"I don't think I can remain friends with Kendra after all that's happened. I should've known something was wrong when she became distant. Lately, she has had nothing nice to say about Marlon. She's only been concerned about what was going on in our marriage," Suga said, as she stood in the mirror, brushing her hair.

"I think we should deal with the home front, and see how all of this plays out. It's been real Suga, and trust me I've enjoyed every part of you." I looked her up and down seductively. "I'll miss you, and I hope that you and Marlon can work it out," I said. "Oh, one more thing, let's keep the part about us sleeping together between us. Everything else is a go up until that point."

"Agreed," Suga replied.

Before she left, I gave her a long kiss goodbye. As usual, I allowed her to leave first. We scheduled our sneaky appearances fifteen minutes of one another. I sat back on the unmade bed, stroking my ego. I'd been fucking Marlon's fine ass wife whom I wanted since I'd met her. Marlon thought he was the only man to make love to her. A part of me loved the fact that I had her too.

I was often reminded of the night I witnessed Kendra and Marlon fucking. She called and asked me to meet her at Marlon's apartment, but I'd already been there with one of my bitches. Marlon had gotten drunk and couldn't drive. Kendra was helping Marlon with his plans for Suga's surprise honeymoon. After realizing that Kendra was on her way, I had to finish up and get the hell out of there.

I used Marlon's apartment to bring my girls over for my sexual escapades. I sat in my Lexus down the street and waited. I watched as Kendra pulled into the parking lot and helped Marlon out of the car. After waiting twenty minutes, I went up to the apartment. I approached the door and first checked to see if it was unlocked. The smell of vodka and sweat was thick in the air. Unprepared for what was to come I turned the corner of the foyer, and there they were. Kendra moaned in ecstasy as she rode Marlon's dick on the living room sofa. I pulled my gun from my waist. I always carried it with me, even to the toilet. With my hand shaking and my body filled with anger, I pointed the gun at the back of Kendra's head. I watched as she rode him. With my finger steady on the trigger, I was ready to squeeze. Just moments before spraying the room with bullets, I thought about my unborn child. She just found out she was six weeks pregnant. There was no way I was going to kill my child. My revenge had to wait its turn. I quietly left and waited outside. Fifteen minutes later, Kendra called my phone. Wondering if I should answer, I looked at the caller ID as anger filled my veins. I picked up the phone contemplating exposing her scandalous secret. Kendra asked how far I was from the apartment so I could take her to pick up her car. After a twenty minute wait, I walked back into the apartment to put on my star performance.

"Yo, is this man drunk?" I asked, as I entered the room.

I looked at Marlon as hurt filled my heart. I wondered if he was too drunk to not realize what'd happened.

"Yes. I guess he's been stressing out about the wedding. He wants everything to be perfect for Suga," Kendra said. "Did you know he bought her a house?" she asked.

She grabbed her jacket and purse and prepared to leave.

I should rob this nigga. I know he has some money stashed in here somewhere, I thought.

I was mad as hell and wanted to kill the both of them. Pulling out my gun, I pointed it at Marlon's head as he lay passed out on the sofa.

"What in the hell are you doing? You can't do this shit! He's marrying my best friend in a couple of days," Kendra pleaded as she forced my arm down. "Please Dee, don't do this to Suga."

"Ok, so tell me how we can get his money without killing this nigga?" I asked sternly.

Afraid and nearly in tears, Kendra stood in shock with her hands over her mouth. I knew her trifling ass wouldn't take long to come up with a scheme.

"We can blackmail him. He doesn't know what the hell is going on, right? I can tell him that we had sex, and I'm pregnant by him. Come on, we both know this isn't his baby," she said convincingly.

She had no idea that I'd seen the two of them fucking just minutes earlier. I questioned if the baby was mine.

I could've killed both their asses, I thought as I looked at her with anger filled eyes.

"How in the hell is that going to work? I guess you have all that figured out, huh?" I asked, avoiding the hidden truth.

"No, but I will come up with something," she said. She paced the floor. "He loves Suga too much to lose her so I'm sure he will give me anything I ask for to keep me quiet," she said.

I agreed with her plan. I knew they would both see karma's kiss. Trust was a thing of the past in our marriage.

After our daughter was born, I convinced Kendra that we should get a paternity test. After altering it, we used it to blackmail Marlon. He was too smart to take Kendra's word, so the test was the proof we needed. I wanted the paternity test to be sure that Destiny was mine. If I'd found out she wasn't, there was no need for Kendra to live.

Using her great office skills, the test appeared to be authentic enough to convince Marlon. If I didn't know the true test results, I would've believed that he was the father.

I had plans of my own for them. Suga was committed to Marlon, and I knew it wouldn't be easy to gain her trust. The way I figured it, once I told her about our cheating spouses the rest would be a piece of cake. Knowing Suga's fragile state, I would be careful and lay that type of hurt on her gently. I knew things could go left if I didn't handle her right. It wasn't long before my mission was accomplished.

CHAPTER 28

Suga

I returned home expecting to see Marlon at the house. After pulling into the driveway, I noticed his truck wasn't there. I reached into my bag for my cell phone to see if I had any missed calls. There were two new text messages and one was from Marlon. After reading the text, I was relieved to know that I had time to shower. Headlights shined from a car that pulled into the driveway as I was walking up the sidewalk to the door. As I tried to get a clearer view, I heard the sound of the car window roll down. When a face became visible, I realized it was Teesa.

I turned and continued to walk to the house. As I opened the front door, she walked in behind me. It was awkward standing in front of her, knowing that she was my mother after thinking she was Sable. A few days had passed since our argument, but I did want to talk to her. I was curious to know what happened back then. I wanted closure, and it was what I needed.

"Hi, honey. I've been so worried about you," she said, as she reached to hug me. "How are you feeling?" She searched my face for marks or bruises.

"I'm fine. I've had a lot on my plate. After finding out about you, I now have many unanswered questions. I don't know where to begin. Lately, I've thought about going to see my dad."

I watched her body language change.

"I know you've had questions for me and I will answer every single one of them. It's only fair that you finally know the truth about the events that led up to that day. Once I've done that, I think you'll understand why I made my choice. It wasn't the best decision, but being in love makes you do some strange things."

"I want to know what happened. I need closure. Please tell me everything, mom. I'm ready," I said. I walked to the kitchen table.

As I sat down, I took a deep breath and braced myself.

She sat down at the kitchen table next to me. I walked to the stove and prepared some tea. Although I'd told her I was ready for the story, I knew that walking down memory lane would be difficult. I noticed tension in her body.

"Would you like a lemon wedge?" I asked, as I placed the cups on the table.

"Yes, thank you," she responded.

I joined her at the table. She'd held it all in for years so releasing it would be far from easy.

"A week before your father was arrested, his wife

approached me at his lounge. She accused me of being with her husband. I had no idea what she was talking about. In my mind I knew I wasn't sleeping with another woman's husband. I told her she must've been mistaken and had me confused with someone else," she explained.

"My father was married? That explains why he was never there with us," I said, shaking my head in disbelief.

"I thought she was some chick who was drunk because I'd been with your father for years and only him. I wanted to beat her ass, but I was trying to give her drunken ass a pass," she said, as she took a sip of her tea. "Then, she rambled and screamed about catching me at a hotel with him. I knew then she was crazy. I continuously told her that she had me fucked up, and I didn't know her man. She was positive she'd had me pegged, and that I must've had a twin running around. She mentioned that I had a fake mole on my face," she said.

"Oh my God! Don't tell me—" I said. I put my hand over my mouth in shock.

"That's when it hit me. She thought that I was Sable. I told that bitch that I did have a look alike running around." She squeezed the lemon with anger and tossed the peel on the saucer. "She argued about how he'd left me butt naked at the hotel and went home with her. Sable was a bitch! She'd been fucking your father behind my back," she said angrily while pointing her finger in the air.

"I can't believe she would do something like that to you."

"When they say the truth hurts, they weren't lying. I couldn't believe your father played me like that. When he finally came over and tried to pull us apart, I knew she wasn't lying. That revelation sent a pain through me that hurts still to this day. Before she could get another word out, I leaped over him and punched her in the face. She was laid out in the floor as Linwood stood over her. He looked like a deer in headlights."

There was no way in hell this could be, I thought.

We sat at the table as shock and disbelief came over us. The pain floated over us like a dark cloud.

"I looked at your father and let him know that I knew about his wife and him fucking my sister. I smacked him in the face and kneed him in the groin. There was so much commotion going on that security couldn't handle it. I drew back my fist to get one last blow in, and I was quickly carried out the doors. I left the club that night a changed woman. Heartbroken and hell bent on getting revenge for the betrayal by the two people I loved. I cried all the way home as I rushed to get to you. You were the only one that loved me. I realized all of the years we spent together were a lie. He made me feel like I was going crazy. There were so many red flags, but I was so blinded by love that I failed to see them," she said with regret.

My mother cried as she told her story. I held her hand, letting her know that I was listening, and I cared. We knew that it was time she faced her demons.

"Mom…I never knew all of this was happening. How come you never told me? We use to be best friends."

"I know Suga, but there is more to it. I had to protect you. I did what I thought I had to do for us," she explained.

"You're scaring me, mom. What are you saying?" In fear of her response, I held my breath.

"I'm saying that I think that we need to get a strong drink for this one," she said, wiping her tears.

"Do you still like vodka and cranberry?" I asked, giving her wink.

"You know your momma, girl," she said while laughing.

We were finally restoring our connection, and it felt good. I returned to the table with our drinks in hand. Looking at the photos that were hanging on the wall, she stared at the family photo of us when I was a year old. That was the only picture I had with my father.

"That is one of my favorite pictures," I said, as I watched her rub her fingers around the edge of the frame. "Well, that is the only one with all of us."

"Yes, it is the only one. He never wanted to take pictures, and now I know why," she said with a smirk.

We both sipped from our drinks enjoying the moment.

"Now finish telling me so we can get this out of the way before Marlon comes home," I said, bringing us back to reality.

"Right," she said, sitting her glass on the table.

"Now you're scaring the shit out of me," I said with a nervous laugh.

"After I found out about Sable and your dad I lost it. I wanted to kill your aunt, but I didn't want to go to jail and lose you. I confronted her the day before the party. That bitch believed she did nothing wrong. She felt I was dumb for not knowing before then. She showed no remorse, and that sent me over the edge. I wanted her dead. I believed she crossed the line, and there's no turning back from it. I laced some cocaine and gave it to her. I wanted her to hurt, but once everything happened I panicked and here we are," she said like it was a walk to the candy store.

"Oh my God! Now I remember the both of you arguing the night before."

"I didn't know what to do when I watched her collapse. Although I wanted her dead, I was afraid and decided to run. I'm so sorry that I killed her because I now know I could've chosen to sever all ties. I beat myself up every day for what I did to her. Most of all, I left you Suga and I'm so sorry," she said, as she reached for my hand from across the table.

The front door opened, and Marlon came in with an arm full of bags. We jumped up from the table as if we were caught with our hands in the cookie jar.

"Hey, I thought I would bring something home for dinner," Marlon said, looking at us strangely.

"Thanks, honey. Give us a minute," I said, greeting him with a kiss and removing the bags from his arms.

Marlon went upstairs to give us privacy.

"Mom, trust me, this is between us," I whispered. "I'm so glad that you came back and most of all I thank you for telling me the truth. I understand, and I'll take care of you. Don't worry about anything. I love you, mom," I whispered into her ear while we hugged.

I felt the weight lift off of both of us while we were embraced. Although a crime was committed, I didn't want her to be brought to justice. I knew all of her problems weren't solved, and murder was one that would never go away. I knew she'd hide for the rest of her life.

CHAPTER 29

Dee

I met Marlon at the club. The doors opened at ten o'clock, and the lounge was available to V.I.P. customers. Usually, we would meet there to discuss business, but that day it was personal. We sat in silence for the first couple of minutes.

"How are the investments?" Marlon asked to break the ice.

"We're making profits as usual. One of our stocks is down, but we're going to get back right," I said calmly.

"Cool. Did you find out what I needed?" Marlon asked.

"I did, but I'm not sure that you want to hear this shit." I popped open the wine bottle. "I don't know how to tell you this…but," I said, as he leaned over towards me.

"Don't fuck with me. I asked you a question, and I'm waiting for an answer," Marlon asked impatiently.

I rose from my seat and shook my head. "Like I said, I don't think you're ready for this."

"I already know. I want to hear it from you, my nigga. We go way back before bitches and money, right?" Marlon questioned.

I became uneasy. I wasn't sure what we were talking about anymore.

"Sit the fuck down," he demanded.

His demanding tone made me think about pulling out my gun. For years, I was Marlon's shadow while I took all of the risks. Without receiving any credit, I ate what he gave me. I was tired of it. Loyalty held my position, but it was a new day.

"You want to do this? Right here, right now?" I asked. I returned the look.

Not wanting to jump the gun and say the wrong thing, I allowed Marlon to lead the confrontation.

"She told me everything, man. I know you've been holding out on me. You're supposed to be my man. Why didn't you tell me what that bitch was into?" he asked.

"You're talking about L.C., right?" I asked with uncertainty.

"Yeah, what the fuck did you think I was talking about? I figured Kendra with her big ass mouth told you everything. I figured she knew," Marlon said.

Letting out a sigh of relief, I know it didn't go unnoticed.

"It didn't come from Kendra. My dude at the barbershop gave me the drop on it. I don't think Kendra knew about Suga being a lesbian. He was there the night it went down and saw the whole thing. He knows L.C. from around the way," I informed Marlon.

"If I had known that shit a long time ago, we could've had some fun," Marlon said, giving me a handshake.

SNOOK

The crowd picked up in the club, and since we weren't there on business so to speak, we needed to move things along quickly. Marlon signaled for the hostess as she walked over to our table and handed me a large envelope.

"Marlon, are you sure this is what you want? It still doesn't change what happened," I said, placing the envelope in my inside jacket pocket.

"I know what I'm doing, Dee. I get the feeling that if I don't handle this now, it won't be the last time she hooks up with her. That's my wife, and I'm getting rid of anything in the way. That's just how it's going to be from here on out," Marlon said.

CHAPTER 30

Suga

*M*arlon returned home with dinner from my favorite restaurant, *Croaker's Spot*. The two piece fish boat, fried potatoes, and cornbread were my favorite. It was more than enough for the two of us. I'd been craving that meal more than usual lately.

"Hey baby, where are you? I bought your favorite," he called out.

Unable to answer him immediately, I could hear his footsteps echo through the hallway. As I heard him approaching the bedroom door, I responded faintly.

"Marlon, I'm in here honey," I said, kneeling over the toilet in the bathroom.

"Baby, what's wrong? Are you okay?" Marlon asked, as he kneeled down next to me.

I moved my hair out of my face to avoid the vomit that erupted from my stomach.

"I've been sick all day," I said. I wiped my mouth. "I haven't been able to keep anything down," I said, heaving as he rubbed my back. "Baby, I'm so sorry I ruined our night."

"Suga, that doesn't matter. I just need to make sure that you're okay," he said with concern.

Marlon reached for a hand towel and wet it with warm water. He helped me off of the floor and to the bed. After pulling the covers back, Marlon helped me to bed. He placed the warm towel on my forehead. For a moment, it seemed the lies, deceit, and betrayal we'd experienced was no longer relevant.

"Thanks, baby. I don't know what happened. I feel a little better now that I've hugged the toilet," I said embarrassed by my actions.

"Let me fix you some warm tea. I bought you home a fish boat, but I guess you don't want it now," he said teasing me.

"I've been craving that for a couple of days and now I can't have it," I said while fluffing the pillows behind me. "Just put it in the microwave, and I will try to eat it later."

The familiar symptoms gave me a strong indication that I was pregnant again. Experiencing morning sickness more than a couple of times, I knew I was pregnant. I promised myself that this time would be different. After all that Marlon and I had been through, it was a good time to have his child. My mind wondered about the fact that there was a strong possibility that the baby could've been Dee's, but it didn't matter. I planned on raising the child as Marlon's. I didn't care about the baby's paternity.

That was the only answer to our marital problems.

Although I was pregnant, it didn't change the fact that Marlon had a daughter that we loved. In reality, I wouldn't be the first to give birth to his child, and it hurt. I knew it was my fault that I wasn't the first.

I planned on talking to him about the Kendra situation so we'd both could be free of the lies. It was only fair that I called his bluff. I was exposed in the worse way, and I planned to even the playing field. Dee said he would talk to Kendra, but I was unsure if he'd go through with it. Several minutes later, Marlon returned with a cup of tea and crackers on a tray.

"Here baby, sit up and eat these crackers," he said.

"Thanks. There was something that I wanted to talk to you about," I said hesitantly.

"What's up?" he asked in a tensed tone.

I took a deep breath and looked down at the tea and crackers.

"I know this may be hard to understand, but my Aunt Sable is really my mom Teesa."

I watched Marlon's body language change as he poured the tea into my cup.

"She admitted it to me while I was there. I always knew that there was something familiar about her all these years. Initially, I was mad, but last night we spoke about everything and I feel like we can work on getting things back the way they were," I confided in Marlon.

"What?" he asked in a confused tone. "What in the hell are you talking about? Let me take your temperature," he said, as he walked into the bathroom and looked for the thermometer. "You must have a fever or something because you're talking crazy," he said, as he placed his hand on my forehead.

SNOOK

"Boy, I don't have a fever," I said, snatching his hand off of my forehead. "I'm serious and you're playing around. She really is my mother," I said, slightly raising my voice.

"How? I thought your mom died years ago," he said, as he sat back down on the edge of the bed.

"No. Apparently it was my Aunt Sable that died that day. Baby, I know this is confusing, but I can't tell you everything right now. Just trust me okay," I said. I held his hand. "You have to promise me that you'll keep this between us. I mean it. Just continue pretending that she is my aunt. She didn't want me to tell anyone and that included you. She could get into a lot of trouble behind her identity being revealed."

"You have to explain to me how in the hell your aunt is your mother," he said. "I don't understand and after all that you've been through. You've dealt with a lot since her death," Marlon replied now pissed off after reminiscing on all of my fainting spells and anxiety attacks. "I hope she gave you a better reason than you're giving me," he said angrily.

Marlon fell back on the bed with his hands on his face. I turned to him and looked directly into his eyes. Against me and my mother's sworn secrecy, I told Marlon everything that she shared with me. Marlon couldn't believe the story I shared regarding my mother, aunt, and father. It did sound like something off of a daytime soap opera. I could tell Marlon was unsure of believing the crazy story, but after swearing him to secrecy I assured him that Teesa was alive and well.

"Now that she's back, I was thinking about going to see my dad," I blurted out.

"Just because your mom rose from the dead doesn't mean

you're going to have this big happy family," Marlon said. "I don't want you to set yourself up to get hurt again. You're a grown woman now, and they're the ones that missed out. Hell, she was wrong for leaving you like that period!"

"I know, but I think that it's time that I go see him. After talking to her, I know that there was nothing that he could've done for me. I'm not mad at him anymore. Uncle Redd did a great job raising me, and I'm thankful for that. I just want to see what he has to say," I said, as I slipped a cracker into my mouth. "Besides, he gave me a key and I don't know what it's for."

"A key? You have to see him about a damn key?" Marlon asked while shaking his head. "Suga, do what you feel you need to do, but I think that it's some bullshit. This man has been locked down for some crazy shit, and he has never tried to contact you. Not that I know of," he replied.

"First of all, it wasn't that he didn't want to contact me. Uncle Redd didn't allow him to write or allow me to visit him in prison. He thought it would've been too much for me at the time. He was right, it would've been. You don't know what I've been through, Marlon," I said, now raising my voice. "Uncle Redd didn't tell me he and my dad spoke all the time. He'd call, and Uncle Redd would tell him how I was doing and I never knew it," I said while wiping the tears from my eyes. "I thought he'd forgotten or didn't care about me. I knew he loved me when Uncle Redd gave me a package that he sent. That was when he gave me some money and the key," I said while overwhelmed with emotion.

"Like I said, it's up to you, but just know that I'm not feeling this shit at all." Marlon was unfazed by my explanation of why I wanted to see Linwood. "You've said that your aunt and mom are identical twins. What if that's your crazy ass aunt trying to pose as your mother? She might be trying to get money from you or something. She sees how you're living and maybe she wants a piece. Come on now, Suga! Think! Don't be stupid!"

"So you think I'm stupid?" I said while rolling my neck with attitude. "Good night, Marlon. I'm going to see my dad tomorrow, and that's that!"

CHAPTER 31

Linwood

The corrections officer called my name, alerting me that I had a visitor. This was unusual since I demanded no visits from anyone on the outside. Life or death circumstances were the only reasons why I'd see someone. Doing prison time meant you had to disconnect yourself from the outside world. I couldn't take having my heart ripped out every week after a visit, so that had to be avoided. On my walk to the visiting room, I was reminded of a scheduled visit from my lawyer. We were to discuss my appeal, so I assumed that was who I was being escorted to see. I was taken to the family visitation area. I knew then; it wasn't my lawyer.

When I got to the visiting area, I looked around for my lawyer as the corrections officer patted me down. I was unshackled, and the handcuffs were removed. I rubbed my wrist as the circulation flowed freely. As a sense of urgency came over me, I continued to scan the room for another familiar face. I didn't immediately see one. As I glanced each direction, to the far right was a beautiful young lady. Not immediately sure of her identity, her presence made my nerves flutter uncontrollably. My heart pounded harder inside of my chest. The corrections officer led me over to the beautiful face with eyes like mine. The closer I got to her, the more the lump in my throat was hardened by fear. I couldn't believe it was Suga, my beautiful daughter.

Suga sat nervously bouncing her leg up and down as she sat and looked around the room. That was the first time she'd ever been to a correctional facility, and would probably be her last after the security check. The cheap makeover the room had was painted in bright green shades. Unfortunately, nothing could disguise the staleness in the air. There were two rows of chairs facing the security desk with small tables where inmates sat for visits with their loved ones. A play area for the children was set up to help the visits feel more comfortable.

I became nervous as I wondered about the lies she'd been told about me. With tear-filled eyes, we stared at one another for several minutes. Although we were father and daughter, we were strangers. I admired her beauty that reminded me of the love of my life.

"Suga, I can't believe it's you," I said, as I reached for her hand. "What made you want to take such a long trip to see an old man?" I asked tearfully.

"It's been a long time, huh? I wanted to see you. How are you?" she asked with concern.

"Don't worry about me. How are you? The last I heard you'd gotten married. Have you two made me a grandfather yet?" I asked jokingly.

"No kids yet, but I'm hoping soon. I've had some recent changes in my life, and I need some closure. All these years I've been living a lonely life without you and my mother. I've made a mess of things because of it. Trying to make things right is the reason for my visit," she explained.

"What type of closure are you seeking?" I asked not, knowing what she'd been told her entire life. "Your mother is dead and I'm here wasting away. What more are you looking for? You have to live for you, Suga. Don't let your past dictate your future, not unless you want to fail. I'm here for you and always will be. I know you may think that I abandoned you, but I didn't. Your Uncle Redd has always been protective of you and thought that it was best that we didn't have contact. I respected that, and now realize that it was probably the best thing for you at the time. Over the years, he shared your biggest moments. He even sent me pictures of you while you were growing up," I said, as I smiled with pride. "I love you, Suga. I need you to stay strong. You're all I've got left."

"Uncle Redd didn't tell me any of this until I was older. By that time, I already felt abandoned and unloved. The pain had set in. You have no idea what I've gone through. When my mom died—" she said, trying to muster up the words.

The last thing that I wanted to do was bring up Teesa. I knew the pain of losing her was too much for me so I couldn't imagine what it was like for Suga.

"Baby, I've been waiting a long time for this. I love you so much," I said, as I poured my feelings out on the stainless steel table. "I don't know what you've been told, but you're my one and only child. I loved your mother, and whether she believed it or not, she was the love of my life. I'm not going to deny the fact that I was married when we met. No, I didn't tell her and that was where I fucked up. I was young back then. Men can do some fucked up shit, even to the ones we love. If I could do it all again, I wouldn't have made half the choices I'd made," I said, as tears continued to fill my eyes.

Trying to read the thoughts that ran through Suga's mind was difficult. She sat in silence and often looked away. She watched as the little ones played, while their parents held hands and made every moment count. Others allowed their body language to show that they didn't have a pleasant visit. The couple next to us argued about the previous week's visit.

Suga searched for the truth as she looked deeply into my eyes. At that point, there was no reason for me to lie. The past was the past, and if we were ever to move forward, it was time to put the past behind us. An officer walked over to warn us our visit would soon end.

"I don't know when I'll be able to come back to see you, but I would love to hear something from you. There was something else I had to ask you. What does the key you sent me belong to?" she asked while leaning towards me.

"It's the key to my life's work," I said. I gave her a wink. "I have no one on the outside that I trust but you. I've been burned by many. One of those people was your mother, but I deserved it. I trust that you'll do right by me," I told her while looking over my shoulder to see if the corrections officer was watching.

We stood up when the officer walked towards us.

I reached for Suga to embrace her and whispered, "I love you."

Suga smiled but didn't say it back to me.

It was okay that she didn't, and I didn't expect it. That was the first and maybe the last time I'd see her while inside those walls. I was fine with that idea since I'd worked on getting home sooner than later.

CHAPTER 32

Suga

A fter leaving the prison, my body reminded me of my condition. It was screaming pregnant loud and clear. I was anxious to get a pregnancy test but wanted to feel Marlon out first. With our marriage still in question, I had one other thing to tell him. Letting him know that I knew about him fathering Kendra's daughter would not be easy.

How can I expose him without exposing myself? I thought on the long trip home.

I knew that I needed evidence. Marlon could deny that he had sex with Kendra, which could allow him to deny being the father of her daughter. The lies we lived made me sick.

I planned to meet Teesa at the house and Kendra for a girl's night out. I wanted to get the pregnancy test out of the way, but I realized it had to wait. My mother was in the driveway when I arrived.

"Hi. I thought we were supposed to meet an hour ago," she said with worry.

As we walked to the door, she looked at me strangely. I wasn't sure if I should tell her where I'd been or what Linwood and I discussed.

"I've been busy all day, so I lost track of time. Besides, I didn't have phone service where I was," I explained as we entered the house.

"Where did you go today?" she asked curiously.

I took a deep breath and looked at her.

"I went to see my father. Mom, he is still grieving over you," I said, as I looked for a sign of remorse.

"What? Why did you do that?" she asked. She walked around the kitchen table with anger filled eyes. "You didn't tell him anything did you?" She paced and rubbed her hands together.

She peeked out of the window and closed the blinds. Her paranoia had taken over in a matter of seconds.

"No, I haven't told anyone. I told you that I understood how important it was that no one knew. I don't want to lose you again," I said, embracing her.

While embraced, I could feel her heart racing.

"I have something that I need to talk to you about. I don't know how you're going to take this. If you're anything like me we could be on the run," she said. She gestured for me to take a seat.

"What is it?" I asked nervously.

"Well, I think that you're a stepmom and I found out that Marlon has a—"

SNOOK

Interrupting her, I held my hand up. Hearing the words made it hurt even more. I'd been feeling inadequate and foolish for staying with Marlon, and continuing to be Kendra's friend. I realized how dysfunctional the situation was.

"Mom, I know. How did you find out?"

"I went to talk to him at the store and overheard him and Kendra arguing about it. I couldn't believe it. I thought that he loved you," she said, as frustration and confusion filled her face. "We had a fight and I gave him a piece of my mind. I'm sure he knows that I might have said something to you by now. Has he been behaving strangely lately?" she asked.

"No, not really. Please don't interfere in my marriage again. Besides, I haven't been feeling well, so he has been very attentive. With all that's been happening lately between us, I doubt if he will be confessing to anything," I said, as the thoughts of my past played out in my head.

"If you two love each other no one should be in pain. That's what got me into the situation that I'm in," she said. She hit her hand on the table. "I don't know how in the hell you're still with a man that fathered a child with another woman. You two haven't had children of your own yet."

"I'm dealing with it. We're going to get through this," I said defensively. "My way is the way it's going to be."

"Have you been having an affair?" she asked, as she looked at me with piercing eyes.

Shocked by the question, I didn't know how to respond. Tired of lying, I had to be freed of it all.

"Sort of, but I don't love him," I said. I looked away and avoided eye contact. "We found comfort in one another. I thought it would make me feel better, but it didn't. It was bad enough that he caught me having sex at the club. All of this is a mess, and I want everything out in the open. Hopefully, we will be able to move on with our lives. I want to raise our child together as a family. I want that more than anything now," I said, as I looked for a reason to make things right.

"Are you pregnant?" she asked as her body language changed. "Are you?"

She placed her hands on my stomach.

"I think so," I said, as I placed my hands on top of hers. "I haven't taken the test yet, but I'm sure that I am."

"Thank God! That's just what you need, honey. You will be a great mother. I'm sure of it. I guess you have no choice but to work it out, huh?" she asked as her eyes lit up with joy. "Trust me, you don't want to raise a child alone."

"I plan on taking the test tomorrow. I just want to enjoy my night. I'm learning that I have to keep my enemies close. I'm meeting Kendra tonight for drinks."

"The baby's mom? Well, I agree with keeping your enemies close. Take note, sometimes when you think you're playing them they're playing you," she said, as she gazed off in thought. "I can't wait until tomorrow for the test. Let's just get one now. I won't get any sleep tonight without knowing for sure." She grabbed her purse and headed for the door.

Driving to the nearest drug store, Teesa parked in front while I ran inside to purchase the test. I was happy to be able to share that moment with my mother. I needed her by my side supporting me. On my way back to the car, I received a text from Kendra making sure that we would still be meeting. I enjoyed my time with my mother, and I didn't want it to end. I had to make sure things appeared normal to Kendra, so I knew I had to meet up with her. If I brushed her off again, she'd be knocking at my front door. She had to be handled with a long handled spoon. The plans I had for her were much more personal. I returned her text advising her that we were still meeting.

When we returned to the house, I immediately took the test. I paced the floor as I waited the longest three minutes as instructed on the back of the box. I knew how to use it, but my nerves made me second guess myself. Thinking back to the other three pregnancies that I didn't go through with I sat in the bathroom each time with shock as I read the positive result while kicking myself. My mother frantically knocked and yelled through the door.

"Girl, are you finished? How long does it say it will take?"

"Please mom, you're making me nervous," I said, as I looked for the double lines to show up. "Calm down out there," I yelled.

"Hurry up, girl! Run some water or something," she said jokingly.

Five minutes passed, and I finally emerged through the bathroom door with my wide-eyed mom waiting for an answer. With the pregnancy test in hand, the smile on my face lit up the room.

"It's positive, mom. I'm pregnant!" I screamed as I jumped up and down.

"Congratulations, baby! I'm so happy for you," she said while hugging me tight.

"I can't wait to tell Marlon. I hope he'll be happy," I said with mixed emotions.

"I'm sure he will be," she said, reassuring me. "Well, let me get out of here so you can go out and celebrate. Call me tomorrow and let me know how it goes," she said, as she kissed me.

"Will do," I replied.

While getting ready, thoughts played in my head on how I would tell Marlon about the baby.

Should I tell Kendra? I thought.

I wondered how much things would change since Marlon and I would finally have a child of our own.

"Hey, girl. I was starting to think that you stood me up," Kendra said.

She stood to hug me, but I quickly took my seat at the table.

"I'm sorry. I was running a little behind. I'm here now," I said, trying not to show disgust on my face.

The hate I felt for Kendra poured out of every fiber in my body. She wanted to be me and live my life. She stooped as low as to be sleeping with my man.

"So, what's been up with you? We haven't spoken much lately. Is everything all right?" she asked.

I looked for true concern, but instead I could tell she was digging for information.

"Everything is great. We had a little issue as you know, but nothing will come between me and my husband," I said with confidence. "We all make mistakes, but at the end of the day our love will prevail."

"I know that's right. After all the bullshit Dee put me through we're still standing," she said. "Well, I'm sure that Marlon told you that I resigned. It's nothing personal. I just want to do something different, you know?"

"I understand. You have to do what you have to do. So, what are you going to do now?" I asked, pretending to show interest.

I didn't give a damn what she did or who she did it with. I would make sure it wasn't with my man.

"I want to spend more time with my baby and take some college courses. She is growing so fast, and I don't want to miss another milestone in her life. I registered at V.C.U. for business classes. I plan to be a business owner someday just like you," she said while giving me a wink.

In my head, I rolled my eyes and bit my tongue.

I said, "That sounds like a plan. If you need anything you know I'm here for you,"

The waiter came to our table and took our drink orders. Kendra ordered an Apple Martini, and I ordered a glass of water. Confused by my order, she looked at me strangely.

"A glass of water? Is that all you're drinking tonight? It's our girl's night out, remember? Get a drink," Kendra said while nudging me.

"No, not tonight. I will have water, thank you," I said to the waiter as I looked away.

The waiter looked at us as Kendra and I went back and forth regarding my drink order.

"So, we have an Apple Martini, and a glass of water is that right?" the waiter asked.

"Yes," I responded quickly.

"I know you're not going to have me look like the lush at the table tonight? Since when did you start ordering water? What's up with you?" Kendra asked.

"I just haven't been feeling well. I don't want to upset my stomach and ruin our night. Stop asking so many damn questions. You better be glad that I came," I said jokingly.

Kendra knew me. She probably figured something was wrong, but she let it go. I spent the night avoiding the rest of her prying questions. I provided her with the good and kept the bad to myself.

CHAPTER 33

Marlon

After a long business meeting, we ended up at a bar. It was getting late, so I headed home. Knowing that Suga would probably be upset with me, I crept into the bedroom carefully trying not to wake her.

"What in the hell do you think you're doing?" she asked in a harsh tone. "I thought you would be here when I got back," Suga said. She sat up in the bed.

"Baby I'm sorry, but the meeting ran over. Then I had some business to take care of that couldn't wait," I explained as I leaned in to kiss her.

"I thought business wasn't supposed to come before home," she said while looking at me scowling. "You couldn't call me? You knew I was out. I could've been on the side of the road somewhere," she argued.

Not in the mood for her attitude, I walked to the closet so that I could undress.

"That's why you have roadside assistance," I said jokingly.

A smile quickly took the place of her frown. I always knew how to put a smile on her face.

"Stop playing. Seriously, you should've called and checked on me."

"I'm sorry. It won't happen again. I promise." I climbed into bed, snuggling up to her.

"You ruined my surprise," she said.

"I'm here now and I'm all yours," I told her.

I peeked under the covers to see what she was wearing.

"I wasn't talking about that."

"Then what's the surprise?" I asked, rubbing up and down her legs.

"I'm pregnant," she blurted out as she awaited my response. "What? That's what's up," I said, as I hugged her tightly. "I knew the work that I was putting in wasn't in vain. This time you're going to stay in bed and take care of yourself. You can't stress out on me. All right?"

Excited about the news, I would make sure she had this one. It was time we started a family.

"Marlon, I know about you and Kendra's secret," she said. Her body tensed up.

I could hear her sniffles as her tears hit the pillow like bricks. I sat up in the bed and looked at her in shock. At a loss for words, I searched her eyes and found hate and pain.

"What are you talking about? You know what?" I asked not to give myself away.

"Everything! You know what the hell I'm talking about," she yelled. "I know Destiny is your daughter. You cheated on me with my fucking best friend!"

SNOOK

All the anger and pain quickly came to the surface. I hated to see her hurting. She pushed my hands off of her as she crossed her arms in front of her.

"Hold on Suga, let me explain," I pleaded. I was on my knees begging her for understanding. I figured she expected a lie.

"There's no explanation for what you did! How could you do that to me? I thought you loved me," she said through her tears.

"I'm sorry. I need you to understand that I wanted to tell you when things went down, but I couldn't bring myself to it. That bitch is not your friend," I explained.

"Oh, so that explains why we're still together after that night you caught me at the club. You were on a guilt trip. Bravo!" she said, clapping her hands.

"You're right! I fucked up, and I should've been man enough to tell you. I give you that, but it doesn't excuse what the hell you did to my babies. How in the hell could you kill what we created in love? You took me through that shit for your selfish reasons!"

"So, that's what it took for her to get laid? She fed you lies about me. Her sex was that good that you fell for it?" she asked with a sly chuckle.

"Stop lying to me. I called the insurance company. I never said anything. I'll admit as a woman you have a right to make those choices. I thought that you wanted children."

Standing to my feet, I looked at her.

"I couldn't force you to keep those babies, but with the performances you gave me about having miscarriages you could've won an Oscar."

Suddenly, Suga jumped up and slapped me across my face. I grabbed her arms and pulled her close to me. While holding her tightly, she fought me to break loose from my grip.

"I hate you! Let me go!" she screamed.

"No, I love you. We will get through this," I said, as we embraced while the pain drained through our tears.

I was naked and exposed. Her cries cleansed her soul. She didn't deserve the hell that we had to deal with involving a child outside of our marriage. I held her until she had control of her emotions.

"I'm tired, Suga. I'm tired of this black cloud over our heads. Look, Kendra and I hooked up right before we got married. We were in the middle of planning our wedding and things were crazy. Kendra met me to help with your surprise for the honeymoon. I must've had too many drinks because she drove me back to my apartment. The next morning, I woke up with a hangover and a text from Kendra saying, *"I enjoyed last night. You better not let Suga find out."* She showed up weeks later talking about she's pregnant. She took a paternity test, and when the test came back, it said she was my child. The blackmailing began. She threatened to expose me if I didn't pay. I didn't want something like that to come from her. I didn't want to lose you. So much time had passed, and things had gotten out of control. I have a feeling she's not my daughter," I confessed.

"Why do you think she isn't yours if you had a paternity test?" Suga asked.

"I don't know. It's just a gut feeling I have. Besides, she

had one of those home DNA kits. For all I know she could've lied," I said while everything replayed in my mind.

"You know how Kendra gets down. She can't be trusted," Suga said. She crossed her arms in front of her.

This new information shed light on the situation and Suga seemed to be on my side for the moment.

"I just wanted to be done with it. I didn't have to give her a dime. Dee is her legal father, but I wanted to do the right thing. Suga, I'm so sorry. Please forgive me," I pleaded.

"We both have to forgive. This is going to take time. I'm only worried about the child that I'm carrying. We will move on from here," she said, as she hugged and kissed me.

That was just what I wanted to hear.

"I agree. Take your time and try not to stress yourself. We will deal with Kendra when the time is right."

CHAPTER 34

Suga

After our emotional conversation, Marlon quickly fell asleep. As I lay in his arms tears fell from my eyes. I loved him, but I hated that the two of them betrayed me. I understood that he was a man, and there was a chance that he'd cheat. In my heart, I believed that he did, in fact, love me. He too was flawed.

Knowing that there was a baby growing inside of my womb, I cried myself to sleep. It was painful holding on to my lies about the pregnancies. I cried tears of joy for being given another chance to have a child. I prayed for forgiveness for ending those pregnancies. They weighed heavy on me. I vowed to do all that I could to protect my child. I envisioned a new life with Marlon and our family. With most of the deceit out in the open, I fell asleep with a much lighter heart.

The next morning, I prepared all of Marlon's favorites:

cheese grits, turkey bacon, eggs, toast, and coffee. As we sat at the table, we discussed our plans for the day. I was eager to confront Kendra so that we could put that chapter behind us. We decided to waste no time in inviting her over. Hesitantly, I called her. I made sure she didn't have an excuse not to show up.

"Hey, what are you doing tonight?" I asked.

"I don't have anything planned. What's up?" she asked.

"Marlon is going out tonight so I thought we'd get together. You know how we do it," I said to make it easier for her to agree.

"That sounds good," she replied.

"All right, see you later."

After hanging up the phone, a slight sense of guilt came over me. Setting Kendra up for a confrontation was not my style, but it was needed. I did some cleaning while I played out the confrontation with her in my head. There was a time when I shared all of my secrets with her. There was always the notion that she could throw it all back in my face, but she played her most deadly card. Sleeping with my husband, having a child with him, and telling him about the abortions were boundaries she shouldn't have crossed.

The embarrassment tackled my pride. The thought of what our family and friends would think if they found out that Marlon had a child with another woman tugged at me. I wouldn't be able to provide an explanation. After thinking long and hard about it, I came to the conclusion that having her come over to confront her was the only way. I thought about the *what ifs,* but karma was relentless.

My iPhone alerted me of an appointment I'd scheduled. I walked over to check my phone. There was a notification that I had a doctor's appointment. Focused on Kendra, I'd forgotten that I made my first prenatal appointment. Rushing around the house to get ready, I called Marlon to let him know to meet me at the doctor's office. As usual it went to voicemail. I left him a message, leaving the address.

While getting dressed, I looked at myself in the mirror. I smoothed my white silk blouse over my seemingly bulging belly. I imagined that I was nine months pregnant, which made me smile.

Since it was my first visit to an obstetrician, I didn't know what to expect. I tried to calm myself by taking deep breaths as I pulled into a parking space. I attempted to call Marlon again with no answer. I took a mental note to address that with him later. It felt good to do the responsible thing for my child by seeking medical care.

I signed in at the front desk and took a seat in the waiting room. I looked around as women flipped through magazines and twiddled their thumbs. I looked at them one-by-one as I noticed that they were in different stages of their pregnancies. I watched them go in and out of the door that led back into the exam rooms. I tried to find some form of emotion on any of their faces as I anticipated my name being called. My phone vibrated from a text from Marlon. He informed me that he was in a business meeting and wouldn't be able to make my appointment.

I understood his unavailability. There was still a business to run and money to be made. I felt that I needed to call my mom. She would've loved to have come to the appointment with me. Support was what I needed. The nurse called a name, but the only part that caught my attention was the last name. She struggled to pronounce my first name correctly.

"It's Suga," I said. I stood to my feet.

"Sorry about that. Sometimes I get stumped by these names," the nurse replied sarcastically.

"That's all right," I said, as I approached the door.

The nurse led me to the exam room where I was given a cup with my name on it. She asked for a urine sample, pointed towards the restroom, and instructed me to return to the room when I was finished.

While getting my vitals, the nurse began the twenty-one questions. I watched the nurse as she wrote my life history in my chart.

"What brings you in today?" she asked.

"I'm pregnant," I replied.

"How do you know? Did you take a pregnancy test at home?" she asked.

"Yes, and it was positive," I replied with an attitude.

I told her that this wasn't my first pregnancy. I thought about lying, but it made no sense to deny it.

"How many births have you had?" she asked as she continued to write in my chart.

"None, I had a miscarriage," I answered reluctantly.

"How many miscarriages have you had? Were you advised why you had a miscarriage?" she asked quickly.

I was irritated by the invasive questioning, but I tried to remain calm as I felt attacked.

"I had more than one okay!" I snapped at the nurse.

"Okay, you can discuss any other matters with the doctor. She will be in to see you shortly. Oh, by the way, congratulations," the nurse said dryly while closing the door behind her.

I was left to get undressed and change into a light blue paper gown. The small dull-colored room was cold and on one of the walls was a picture of a womb with a fetus inside. The picture showed the steps of the growth and development of a fetus. Taking deep breaths helped me from passing out. The anticipation of being interrogated was like waiting for the good cop to come into the room. When the doctor came into the room, she made the visit painless. She confirmed that I was twelve weeks pregnant, which was right around the time I began sleeping with Dee. She made an appointment for me to go back so that an ultrasound could be performed. I was all smiles when I left. The ride home made me contemplate the meeting with Kendra. It was bad for all who were involved.

CHAPTER 35

Kendra

hen I arrived at Suga's house, I was taken aback when I noticed that Marlon's truck was in the driveway.

He wasn't supposed to be here, I thought.

Deep inside, I wanted to apologize for the way I'd behaved when I quit weeks before. I got hot thinking about him as I recalled the night that I finally got him to sleep with me. It wasn't just him physically, but the lifestyle he provided for Suga. I fantasized that I would go to meet Marlon for a quick fuck while Suga was out.

I fought the thought that made my center wet. I always regretted not going after the big fish and handing him over to Suga. After all, it was all about the money back then, and I got stuck with the sidekick. I loved Dee, but he was not of Marlon's status. Marlon was the boss and knew how to make the money. I envied Suga and Marlon's relationship and yearned to have that with my husband. I wanted to beat her to the altar and I did, but she wasn't far behind with the bigger prize. No matter what I did, I could never outshine her. She always came out on top. As I walked to the door, she stood waiting for me. I assumed I was watched on her high tech security camera.

"I thought you said this was going to be a lady's night," I said. I gave a nod towards Marlon's truck.

"He's leaving soon. Come on in," Suga said, as she led me inside.

I entered the house and immediately felt the coldness in the air. It was unlike Suga to invite her female friends over when she knew Marlon would be home. She led me into the formal living room, which was normally off limits. I noticed the amazing new artwork that was on the walls. I was sure she had imported it from only God knew where. Like the interior design of the jewelry store, she always had a flare for decorating. The furnishings were all imported with marble and hand carved wooden tables. Red flags were raised by Suga's obviously odd behavior. Something was wrong and where there was smoke there was fire. I prayed I wasn't the one that was going to get burned.

"What the hell is going on?" I asked, standing in the living room, refusing to take another step.

"I think there is something that we should talk about," Suga said.

She took a seat on the leather sofa as Marlon walked into the room.

"What's up?" Marlon asked.

I shot daggers at both of them as I tried to maintain my composure. I contemplated if I should leave or stay.

"Shit, you tell me," I said, shrugging my shoulders. "What in the hell is this, Suga?" I asked as I raised my voice.

"Look, let's all sit down so—" Suga began.

"Sit for what?" I interrupted.

"Sit your ass down! You're in my damn house!" she yelled.

I wanted to curse her ass out and walk the fuck out of there, but against my better judgment I didn't.

"I know that you seduced my husband, had sex with him, and blackmailed him. You did that to keep him under your thumb. Now you're trying to pin your daughter on him. Today all of that ends," she said.

"Seduced him?" I asked, defensively. "I know you don't believe that. He threw himself on me, and I tried to tell him no, but he insisted. He damn near forced himself on me! Don't stand here and lie to her, Marlon! Tell her what happened the night you got drunk," I said. I stood to my feet.

Marlon stared at me with a smirk on his face. It was then I realized I'd walked into an ambush.

"You wanted me from day one," Marlon said, as he looked me up and down. "You saw an opportunity and seized it. I would've never slept with you and you know it! I love my wife and our child."

"Child? You're pregnant?" I asked in shock. "Why didn't you tell me? I thought we were friends," I asked Suga.

"Apparently we aren't friends because friends don't betray each other's trust," she responded coldly.

"You're like a sister to me. You have to believe that *he* is lying to you," I said, as I pointed to Marlon. "It didn't happen the way he claims. We need to talk in private, just me and you. As far as my daughter is concerned, she's well taken care of with all that hush money you gave me," I said. I looked at Marlon.

"What money?" Suga asked with her arms crossed in front of her.

I watched the tables turn as Suga looked at Marlon as another skeleton had fallen out of the closet.

"I didn't give her hush money. It was for the baby. I wanted to do the right thing. Look, none of this mess is the baby's fault. Come on, Suga. Don't let her mess with your head. You know what it is," he said.

Marlon and Suga squared off.

"You didn't tell me you gave her money," she said with anger.

"Like I said, it was for the baby," Marlon replied as he sat back down on the couch calmly.

"Suga, it was his idea to pay me," I interjected. "I didn't ask for anything initially. He offered, so I agreed. I'll admit I did use this whole situation to my advantage at times, but we need to talk about this in private, Suga."

I walked to Suga and took her hand. I wanted to take her out of the room and away from Marlon's grip.

"Bitch, get your hands off my wife!" Marlon yelled, as he yanked my hand away. "She doesn't want to talk to you!"

I grabbed Suga's hand again as Marlon pushed me away. Stumbling backward, I pulled her down with me. He reached for her, but it was too late. She stumbled over me causing her to fall to the floor. Thanks to the large leather ottoman, neither one of us was hurt.

"Marlon, just let me talk to her! What in the hell is wrong with you?" she screamed, while helping me up.

"You better be glad that Suga is pregnant, or I'd kill your ass! Don't you ever put your filthy hands on me!"

Suga held me back.

"Stop! Both of you need to calm down! Marlon, you need to leave. I will deal with you later. Sit down Kendra, and let me deal with you now," she said.

I watched as she walked over to Marlon, advising him to give us some private time. Reluctantly, he decided to leave as Suga walked him to the front door. Everything happened so fast. I needed a drink, so I went into the kitchen and poured me a glass of wine. I sat at the table and cried. The web I tangled was unraveling. I knew our friendship was over and it was my fault.

Suga stood in the doorway and stared at me. It seemed she was trying to read me. Falling apart was her job, and helping her pick up the pieces was mine. In all of the years we'd been friends, I'd never cried in front of her. That day she stood strong when she would have usually crumbled. I noticed a tear fall from her eye.

"I'm fighting against the love that I had for you, and the hate that I now harbor towards you," Suga said, as she slowly walked into the kitchen.

"I'm so sorry. I really am," I said, as I wiped my tears with the back of my hand.

"I don't know if I want to hug or beat the shit out of you

right now," she said. She sat down in the seat across from me. "I need to know what happened and I need to know the truth."

I felt Suga's piercing gaze.

"There's so much you don't know about this situation. I'm sorry for hurting you and Marlon. I know I should've come to you, but I was afraid. Just hear me out," I pleaded.

"Fine," she said. She looked at me suspiciously. "As long as you're not trying to feed me bullshit. I want the truth Kendra, no matter how painful you think it may be. I'm hurt and I'm going to let you say what you need to. Don't forget we're talking about my husband, my life, and my family. That's what you thought you were taking from me, remember?"

"What happened between Marlon and I was a mistake. It's like he said, we met to discuss his surprise for your honeymoon. I was responsible for getting your house ready for you when you guys returned. Marlon got drunk the night we met up. I drove him back to his place. When we arrived, I helped him into the apartment. I didn't plan for any of it to happen, but it did," I said. I hoped she bought it. "It must've been the alcohol. I know he wouldn't have allowed something like that to happen," I told her.

"You fucked my husband and didn't tell me, Kendra! I can't believe you."

"I called Dee and asked him to meet me at the apartment so that he could take me back to pick up my car. Before I knew it, Dee was knocking on the door. By then Marlon was passed out cold, and Dee plotted on how we should rob Marlon. I didn't know what to do. I was afraid. I thought about you and how happy you were with him," I said, as tears fell from my eyes. "I didn't know what Dee would've done so I tried to talk him out of it. He was so angry, and I didn't know why," I said. Suga sat quietly. "Look, my daughter isn't Marlon's. I was already pregnant when it happened. Dee told me to make up the paternity test to blackmail Marlon for money," I admitted as I looked down toward the floor.

I didn't know what would happen next as I waited for Suga's response.

"You selfish, bitch! You fucked my husband and smiled in my face. Oh my God! I can't believe Dee would do that to us."

Suddenly, I watched as she breathed heavily. I recognized the signs of her ongoing anxiety attacks and quickly jumped into action. I gave Suga a glass of water and searched for her pills in the cabinets. Just as fast as it came, it went. She cried uncontrollably.

"Are you all right?" I asked as I stood beside her.

"I don't know. I can't believe all of this is happening," she said in between sobs.

"I'm so sorry Suga, but I know that I saved his life that night. Dee is jealous of him. He scares me sometimes. I know Marlon loves you and would do anything to protect you. I know that's why he did it," I said. "I'm sorry for the role that I played in all of this. I should've been a better friend from the beginning," I said, as I rubbed her back compassionately.

"But, how could you take from me, Kendra? The money Marlon gave you was our money. You know I would've given you anything you needed," Suga said desperately.

"It wasn't about the money for me. I went along with it to protect you. I love you and you know you're my sister. I wanted to tell you a long time ago, but knowing your medical condition I didn't want to hurt you. Please, try to forgive me," I pleaded.

"I will never forgive you!" she said furiously. "I'm mad at myself for trusting a bitch like you. If I weren't pregnant, I would beat your ass. As for your bitch ass husband, you already know how that's going down," she said, as she stared me up and down. "I will not let anything happen to my husband, especially behind your ass," Suga said.

We stood nose to nose. I stepped back and prepared for Suga to swing. If she did, I would've had to whoop her ass, pregnant and all, and pray for forgiveness later.

"Wait a minute," I said abruptly. "I don't think that you should tell him about Dee's part in the scheme. This happened a while ago, and I don't think he would do that to him now. If he wanted to hurt him, he would've done it already. Dee is no longer a threat. I think we should just tell him what I did and that my daughter isn't his. I know you don't want Marlon locked up and leave you to raise your baby on your own do you?" I asked convincingly.

"Bitch please! Get the fuck out of my house," Suga yelled while pointing at the door.

I knew that would be the last time we'd talk. I grabbed my things as I prepared to leave. It hit me that I'd lost my sister.

CHAPTER 36

Redd

The phone rang, and I noticed it was Suga. Excited to see her number, I tried to hurry to answer the call. It had been a while since we spoke. I had been sick with the flu. She was supposed to come over to make chicken noodle soup. I'd gotten worried when she didn't show up as promised.

"Hey, Uncle Redd! How are you feeling?" Suga asked when I answered.

"Hey! I'm doing better. I thought you were coming over the other day?" I asked.

"That's why I'm calling you. I have some good news to tell you. I'm pregnant!" she screamed through the phone with excitement.

"That's wonderful, baby. I know you will be a good mother. I'm happy for you and Marlon. Now it's time for someone else to get spoiled besides you," I teased.

During the brief silence, I thought about how I should've made sure Suga received counseling after her mother's death. Instead, I gave her everything she wanted in hopes it would take away the pain she'd experienced. A psychiatrist would've helped her learn how to channel her emotions in dealing with the loss of Teesa.

"Thanks, Uncle Redd. Umm…I also went to visit Linwood the other day," she said hesitantly.

"I know, he told me. I was waiting on you to tell me," I said, reassuring her it was okay. "One day I knew you would go and see him. I'm glad you've decided to see him. He's wanted to see you for a long time. I thought it was best that we waited until you were ready."

"One more thing, he said something about me holding the key to his life's work. I wasn't sure what he meant. He gave me the key when I graduated. From the stories that I've heard about my father, I know he had money from his business. He's never told me, but supposedly he has a stash somewhere. Do you know anything about that?" she asked.

"Your father was one hell of a businessman. He was very smart, and I'm sure he had money put away. That's something you'll have to discuss with him," I said.

"I guess that's what I will have to do. I'm curious to know what he's talking about."

"I miss your mother so much. Every time I see you, you remind me of her. Having Sable back around makes it hard for all of us. I thought that I could tell them apart, but now I just don't know," I said, as I briefly thought of Teesa.

"I miss her, too."

SNOOK

"I still want that chicken noodle soup. Why don't I send Alyssa over there to get the soup for me? This old man needs to get back on his feet. I have to see my baby girl soon," I said, as I gave a fake cough.

"Sure, I will have it ready for her when she gets here. I love you Uncle Redd, and thanks for taking such good care of me and for being a father to me," she said adoringly.

"I love you too Suga, baby. Thanks for being the daughter I've never had," I said. I felt her loving spirit.

CHAPTER 37

Teesa

I called Suga to see how the doctor's visit had gone. I couldn't wait to find out the due date of my grandbaby.

"Where have you been? I was worried to death!" Suga shouted at me after answering the phone.

"Hello to you, too," I said in shock to her urgent response. "I had to go back home to take care of some business. Sorry, I didn't tell you I was leaving. It was a last minute thing, but I'm back now." I reassured her.

Unfinished business in North Carolina led me back to tie up some loose ends. I'd used Sable's identification and social security number to get a car and an apartment back in North Carolina. The money I'd stolen from Linwood began to dwindle. I had to find another avenue for income. In North Carolina, I was able to find work as a consultant for a neighbor who was an insurance broker.

SNOOK

When I received my first paycheck, I took it to a local bank to cash. The teller advised me that in order to cash the check I had to provide a thumbprint. I didn't have an account at the bank, which required me to provide a fingerprint for identification purposes. Attempting not to make a big deal out of the situation, I quickly became reluctant. Not wanting to draw attention to myself, I placed my thumb in the ink and pressed it on the back of the check. Trying to botch the print, I pressed and moved my thumb around as much as possible.

After a month of working, the neighbor quickly moved. It was never a good sign when someone suddenly left town. I knew the signs all too well. A few days later, the F.B.I. knocked on my door. Nervously, I prepared to come up with a story to explain why my print came back as Teesa and not Sable. Apparently, my employer ran an insurance scam and was being investigated. They weren't there for me, so I answered as much as I could. Not knowing much about him, I didn't have a lot to offer.

Thinking the interview was over, they asked me about the checks that I'd cashed. They stated that the prints on the checks matched a deceased woman named Teesa Johnson. I should've known they would've run the print on the checks since they were investigating a fraud case. Quickly jumping into the character of a grieving identical twin, I explained that my sister died several years back. I voluntarily provided my identification to the FBI agent. The agent was polite and understanding and apologized for the inconvenience. The agent went on to explain how twins shared the same DNA, and it's possible that fingerprints have the same class and ridge characteristics. Luckily for me, the print was too smeared to determine the finer details of the ridges. Considering the circumstances of the case, he decided that I was not the target. He just wanted to question me regarding my relationship with my old neighbor.

I was confident that I satisfied the FBI agent's curiosities, but I couldn't be certain of it. Although I was guilty of it, I didn't want them to come back and accuse me of murder and identity theft. I never anticipated owning up to my crimes at any point.

Regret tormented me at times, but I rationalized it by the fact that Sable had crossed the line. Of all the men that would have loved to have her, she had to have Linwood. Sable's arrogance always upset me. She was the type that said and did what she wanted and made no apologies. When I confronted Sable about sleeping with Linwood she said, "*Damn, it took you long enough. He's a dog. All men are. Why wouldn't he have us both?*"

Sending me over the edge, Sable expected me to lash out at her. That wasn't the time.

I smiled at my twin and said, "Yes, why wouldn't he?"

I was plotting my revenge. I offered her a drink and a line of cocaine. I didn't think about me or my daughter. I was focused on making sure she knew that karma was a mutha. I didn't think that I had it in me, but when I realized what I'd done it was too late. I panicked and fled the scene, leaving behind my life and my daughter.

CHAPTER 38

Suga

After informing me she would move back to Richmond permanently, I offered my mother a room in our home. We discussed her staying around until after the baby was born so that she could assist me after the delivery. I had no idea what to do with a newborn baby, and I knew she would teach me. Reluctantly, she accepted the offer.

I hadn't spoken to or saw Kendra since the confrontation a week prior. I thought about her. I had grown accustomed to contacting her every day, but I was focused on rebuilding my marriage. I couldn't afford for Marlon to find out anything else that could make him leave me.

I turned over to see the clock. It was eight o'clock in the morning. We were all still sleeping when the doorbell rang. I looked at an undisturbed Marlon, who was still asleep. After nudging him, he didn't budge. We weren't expecting anyone so early. I was reluctant to see who was at the door. Cautiously approaching the door, I saw two suited gentlemen with their badges in front of them. I looked down the driveway and noticed two police officers. I looked one of them over, noticing how sloppy his clothing was. His wrinkled suit appeared disheveled.

"Can I help you?" I asked, as I wrapped my robe tightly.

"Yes, ma'am. My name is Detective Wilkes, and this is my partner, Detective Moore. Are you Suga Cole?" he asked.

"Yes, what can I do for you?" I asked nervously.

"Do you mind if we come in?" he asked, "I have some unfortunate news," he said.

"Sure, come in," I replied as I pulled the door open to invite them in.

Detective Wilkes walked into the foyer and pulled out a photo.

"Do you know Ms. Linda Cunningham?" he asked.

Butterflies began to settle in my stomach as I looked at the photo of the familiar face.

"Umm...Yes, I do."

"Her body was found a few days ago in her home along with her companion," he said.

"Oh my God!" I tried to maintain control before I woke up Marlon. "She's dead?" I asked while holding my chest.

"Yes, I'm afraid so. We found several phone calls from and to you in her phone log. Her mother advised us that you two have known each other since you were teenagers. Is that correct?" Detective Moore asked.

"Yes, we were friends for a long time. We've stayed in

contact over the years. I just can't believe that she's gone. Who would want to hurt her? She was the sweetest person and got along with everyone," I said.

I tried to pull myself together, but I was filled with grief. Detective Moore handed me a handkerchief and led me to the living room chair.

"Is there any information you can tell us that may lead to her killer? I know that she lived an alternative lifestyle and shared a residence with her partner. Any information that you may have would help us in this investigation," he said.

"I'm sorry, but I don't know anyone that would want to hurt her. She didn't go around tricking people into thinking she was a man, if that's what you're asking. She looked like a man, but she never lied about being a woman. Do you think that I had anything to do with it?" I asked curiously.

"Well, we're not sure. A friend of hers told us that there were rumors that the two of you were lovers at some point. Is this true?" he asked.

I looked up at the staircase to see if Marlon had gotten up. I looked at the detective with confusion, wondering who could have told him that.

"I'm a married woman and she was one of my best friends. I don't care what you've heard. I don't have anything else to say," I said angrily. I walked him to the door.

Detective Moore looked at his partner with a smirk on his face. I answered the question without answering it at all. As I opened the door, I noticed Marlon standing suspiciously at the top of the stairs. He looked down at us with a smirk on his face. As he walked down the stairs, he didn't say a word.

"I'm going to have to ask you to leave now," I said, as I tried to push the detectives out of the door.

Unclear of how Marlon would respond to the news of L.C.'s death, I was prepared to come up with a story as to why the detectives were there.

"What's going on, Suga?" Marlon asked as he gave the detectives a quick look over.

I explained why Detective Moore and Detective Wilkes were there as the detectives extended their hands to Marlon. Reluctantly, Marlon shook their hands.

"Sorry to hear about your friend, honey. What's for breakfast?" he asked nonchalantly.

Taken back by his response, I knew the detectives thought the same thing I did. Marlon's cold response was a bit rash. Yeah, I know he did catch the two of us in the act, but his reaction led me to my own questions.

"Well, here is my card and if you have anything else to add to this investigation we would appreciate if you call us. Thanks for your time," Detective Moore said, as they walked to the car.

Not wanting to upset Marlon, I closed the door and took deep breaths for several minutes. I had to put on my game face as I walked into the kitchen.

Marlon sat at the table, watching the flat screen that was mounted on the wall. He watched my every move as I prepared breakfast. I privately grieved. I fought back tears. It was apparent he didn't care how I felt.

"Suga, are you done yet?"

I walked the plates to the table as I tried to muster up the words to communicate with him.

SNOOK

"I can't believe that someone killed her. She wasn't a bad person. She didn't deserve to die that way," I said with tears falling from my eyes.

"Are you crying over your girlfriend?" he asked. "I hope you're not shedding tears for the person that I caught you fucking! You're grieving over the same person that almost cost you the comfortable lifestyle that I provide for you. You didn't think that I was going to let the two of you play me like some punk bitch did you? Come on now, I thought you were smarter than that, Suga," Marlon said with a chuckle that gave me chills.

Enraged, I looked at him as though he had confessed to the crime.

"Of course I don't think you're a punk, Marlon. You know what? I always knew there was a monster deep inside of you just waiting to come out. After all these years, when your world is threatened, you show your true colors. I helped you build the company that you pretend to have built by yourself. It's as much my company as it is yours. You can't take all of the credit for this!" I pointed around the house.

Marlon clapped as he leaned back in the chair, admiring my sudden courage.

"Look at you, taking the heat under pressure without falling apart," he said.

I reached across the table to smack him. He grabbed my hand just before it met the side of his face. As he twisted my wrist, I screamed in pain and fell to my knees. He looked down at me as the pain on my face seeped out. Realizing he took things too far, he quickly caught hold of himself.

"Let go of me!"

"Suga, I'm sorry, but you've got me fucked up. I know you didn't think shit was sweet between us. I had to show your ass that this shit is for real so the next time you decide to fuck with someone else you know there will be consequences. You're mine and mine alone. Now get yourself together."

"Is this how you will treat me? By putting your hands on me? You promised you would never do anything to hurt me," I said through sobs.

"I love your ass to death, and I think you know that now," he said with tears in his eyes.

He kissed me on the forehead, walked out, and left me standing in the kitchen alone and confused.

CHAPTER 39

Teesa

waken by a commotion coming from the kitchen, I jumped up, grabbed my robe, and slid on my slippers. I heard a door slam as I hurried to the hallway. The house was usually quiet, and I figured that the commotion was going on between Marlon and Suga. Walking past the master bedroom, I saw that the bed was unmade and empty. I followed the noise down the hall to the bathroom where I found Suga on her knees, vomiting into the toilet. I rushed and grabbed a washcloth and soaked it with water.

"Suga, are you okay?" I asked, as I put the washcloth on the back of her neck.

Her hair was swimming in the toilet.

"No," she cried.

Her red swollen eyes let me know that something was seriously wrong. I'd never seen her so emotional.

"Did Marlon do something to you? If he did, you know your Uncle Redd will be over here in a second. What in the hell did he do?"

"No, it's my fault. Mom, I fucked up bad! Now I'm paying for it." She tried to get up from the floor.

She propped herself up on the edge of the tub with my assistance. She appeared to be weak and defeated.

"What happened?" I asked.

"I don't want you involved in all of this. You have enough going on. I hurt him and he's lashing out on me," Suga said.

She knew I would jump into action if needed.

"I'm going to tell you now, in case you don't already know, but the first time I see some crazy shit going on between you two it will be the last. Do you understand me? I've never tolerated a man putting his hands on me, and I for damn sure am not going to tolerate a man putting his hands on my child," I said sternly.

I briefly thought about a time when Linwood smacked me for questioning him. He'd been out and came in at five o'clock in the morning. Before I knew it, I was on the floor holding the side of my face and sucking a bloody lip. In a matter of seconds, he stood gasping for air as I stood with a butcher knife held against his throat. That was the last time he ever hit me. I'd always shared with Suga that love would never hit you. The day Linwood hit me was the day I should've left. I felt the blame riding my back as I looked at my hurting daughter. If I were there, I could've taught and shown her better. How could I show her how to be a strong black woman after running away from my problems?

SNOOK

I sat down beside her as I admired how beautiful she'd grown to be. Suga was the most beautiful baby I'd ever seen. She had the prettiest complexion and the dreamiest eyes. It was like her eyes looked right through to your soul. Linwood cried when he first laid eyes on her.

"I will do anything for you, even if that means losing my freedom. I have no one else to blame, but myself for the decisions that I've made in my life. I'm not going to let you make the same mistakes I made. You have a lot of my characteristics in you, and it scares me," I said regretfully.

"Everything is going to be fine. He didn't hurt me. We had a fight, and that's all. We love each other, and we'll get through this," she said, trying to convince me. "It's my fault as I told you."

"I love you, but you have to love yourself first. You have to know that you're worth more than this. This big house, the cars, and clothes don't define who you are. You can't allow Marlon and his money to dictate how you feel about yourself. If you don't think he loves you the way you should be loved, then you love yourself that much more. You're pregnant with a child that needs your love. You must love your child more than yourself. If I would've done that a long time ago then we—"

"How in the hell can you tell me anything about love or about what my child needs?" she interrupted. "You can't say shit to me about anything. You didn't love me. You just loved yourself, and that's why you're in the predicament that you're in now. My child will be loved, and I will never leave my child like you left me. Why did you really come back?" she asked angrily.

It was apparent Suga's issues were far beyond my reach. I knew I made mistakes, but I wasn't going to stand for her disrespect.

"I don't want you to take this the wrong way, but I came back because I had to. My reasons for leaving were selfish, but I realize now that you're what is most important in my life. Yes, I fucked up, but we have to move past it. I'm sorry and yes I'm running out of money and time. I spent most of my time running for my life and trying not to shame my family, because of my choices," I explained.

We shot painful glares at one another. We were both hurt by one another's words.

"No matter what, I'm your mother. I will always love you and my grandchild." I left Suga standing in the bathroom.

"Mom I love you, too. I get upset when I think about the times you weren't there!" she yelled down the hall.

I didn't respond to Suga's final statement. I continued to my room as her words met its target, my heart. Tears fell from my eyes as the pain from her words pierced me. I fell to my knees and wept loudly. I vowed to do all that I could to make up for lost time, and the pain that I caused her.

CHAPTER 40

Suga

I feared for my marriage more than ever, and it was evident that Marlon had changed. When he looked at me, it wasn't with love. It was with disgust. He was considered to be a dangerous man, and I no longer trusted him. If the marriage failed, I'd have nothing, and I refused to let that happen. I would have a child that needed to be cared for, and there was no way I would struggle to take care of my child.

I had to do something about the mess I got myself into. How could I be so dumb, and trust a snake like Dee? All I had to do was talk to my husband, but instead I slept with the enemy. There was still the possibility that he could be the father of my child. Moving on with my life would be difficult, and I had to pick up the pieces one by one.

Months passed, and I still hadn't returned to the office. I found it more relaxing to work from home since Kendra was no longer employed at the store. As I sat at my desk, I looked over months of invoices. This was the unfinished paperwork that needed to be completed that I'd started before my nightmare began. At the end of the day, I was still a businesswoman.

After crossing the *T's* and dotting the *I's*, I took my monthly allotment from the business account. Although I shared the business responsibilities with Marlon, I didn't get paid regularly. That was the way Marlon wanted it. He provided everything, but I wasn't satisfied. I rolled with it for the sake of argument. Instead, I paid myself under my consulting business. Consulting with Marlon was enough to enable me to save a pretty penny. A woman must have a rainy day fund because it was sure to not only rain but pour one day. I was good at saving money. I didn't have a need to spend any of it.

I handled the taxes, which gave me access to the main business account. Since Marlon never looked over any of the paperwork, I had full control of how the business was maintained. The only thing he was concerned with was his private books. I wasn't privy to that, so I didn't mind that he kept them from me. Besides, the less I knew, the better.

CHAPTER 41

Marlon

I arrived to work early so that I could get some work done. The store was already opened. I glanced up at the camera and noticed trouble entering the store. I quickly walked to the front of the store.

"What the hell are you doing in my store?" I asked as I approached Kendra.

I'd recognize her round hips and perfectly thick thighs anywhere. As much as I hated her, I wanted to know what she'd told Suga. Suga refused to discuss what happened between them. It seemed that ever since I'd aired out my dirty laundry, shit began to backfire. I wasn't sure where we stood.

"I'm here to pick up Dee's ring. I'm not here for your tired ass. Is it ready yet?" Kendra asked rudely.

Embarrassed by the whispers from her former co-workers, she sucked her teeth as she realized that they all knew how scandalous she was. They witnessed it first hand when Suga wasn't around. I watched as she bit her nails and scowled at them.

"Dee knows that shit won't be ready for another couple of days. I know he didn't send you in here for that. So why the hell are you here?" I asked.

"What? Just call him when it's ready. I don't know why the hell he sent me here," she complained.

"Me either," I responded as I walked out of the store.

Kendra exited the store behind me.

"That was some fucked up shit you pulled. You knew what the hell you were doing that night. You weren't that drunk. Why in the hell would you try to throw me under the bus? That's all right. If Dee ever finds out about it, he will kill your ass," she replied as she switched down the street to her car.

"Fuck you and Dee. He knew he married a slut. I told him that he couldn't turn a hoe into a housewife," I said. I took a long pull off my cigarette.

"Fuck you and that weak ass bitch, Suga," she said, as she flipped me off and got into her car.

I turned to walk back towards the store, and there was Gooch.

"What's up, Gooch?" I asked giving him dap.

I noticed Gooch looking closely at Kendra.

"What it do? Who is that?" Gooch asked as he continued to watch her as she pulled off.

"That's Dee's girl, Kendra," I said suspiciously. "I got work to do my man," I said. I gave him a handshake and walked back into the store.

I left Gooch standing on the sidewalk. Anytime Gooch was around; he was sure to leave a body behind. Gooch was called the *Grim Reaper* in the hood. He was an old head, but a well-respected one. He made his living as a hit man, and he robbed and got high. He was public enemy number one. I knew first hand since I'd used him a few times in the past.

If Gooch was there on business, he was stalking his prey as he was known to do. I wasn't sure who the victim was, but I wasn't sticking around to find out. Noticing others taking cover to avoid Gooch's presence, the sidewalk that was once filled with people was empty. You may see Gooch once, maybe twice, but if you see him a third time you better run for your life.

CHAPTER 42

Dee

We were home alone for the first time in a long time. Ever since the baby was born, our world revolved around her. We neglected one another, and I didn't mind at all. I had women lined up, so it didn't become an issue.

"How come you and Suga haven't gone out lately?" I asked Kendra.

"Baby, please don't ruin our night by talking about that bitch again. I told you that I don't fuck with her anymore. Anytime she has to go around spreading lies about me you're not my friend," Kendra replied defensively. "Why? Did Marlon say something to you about it?" she asked.

"No, but we haven't kicked it like we use to. I don't know. I thought maybe it had something to do with you two."

I watched Kendra cut into her perfectly cooked steak.

SNOOK

She'd been avoiding the conversation by using our daughter as a distraction.

"Now, what did Suga do? I know you're not going to let some *he said, she said* shit come in between you two," I said, as I poked at my steak.

I knew Suga must've mustered up the nerve to say something to Kendra. It had been long enough, but I figured I'd better take what I could get. I was tired of taking my anger out on other women. That was getting old.

"If this was supposed to be a romantic dinner, you're killing the mood with this bullshit. Don't worry about me and Suga. That's our business so let's talk about something else," she said in an annoying tone.

"Yeah, let's do that," I agreed.

I felt it was the perfect opportunity to bring out our skeletons.

"Listen to me and don't say a fucking word. I saw you and Marlon that night at his apartment. Do you know how close I came to killing your ass?" I asked, taking a bite of my steak.

Looking at me with fear in her eyes, I was convinced she was going to find a way to get out of it.

"I knew it! You were there! I couldn't figure out why you were so angry. Now it all makes sense."

We looked at one another from across the table. Tension ran deep between us.

"I'm sorry, Dee. I don't know what the hell happened that night. That was the biggest mistake of my life," Kendra pleaded.

"That's what I had to believe all this time for me not to hurt you. I always knew you settled for me, but Marlon wouldn't have chosen you. You would've just been another notch on his belt. I loved you even when you were out there scouting for the next come up. If it weren't for my daughter, you wouldn't be here right now. I put that on our daughter's life."

I exhaled as I felt the weight climb off of my shoulders within minutes. I'd finally let out the feelings that I'd harbored for so long.

"Baby, I'm so sorry. I never meant to hurt you. I love you," Kendra said, as she walked towards to me.

Suddenly, the front door chime alerted the alarm. I stood to my feet as I patted for my gun. After realizing it was in the bedroom, I thought about the one I'd hidden in the living room. Trying to figure out how I would get to it, Kendra froze with fear. She covered her mouth to avoid a scream from escaping.

"Stay here," I whispered as I peeked around the corner.

As I entered the front room, the door was slightly opened, letting in the moonlight. I heard footsteps behind me where I left Kendra. I swung around to find her. I let out a sigh of relief.

"I told you to stay in the kitchen. I got this," I whispered as I pulled her close to me.

I wanted to get her out of the house. I was sure we were being robbed. Whoever had the balls to come for me, I was sure they knew they would have to kill me.

"Follow me to the front door and keep quiet," I whispered.

Hearing nothing in the house but our heavy breathing, I tried to listen for some other movement. Moving along the wall down the hallway, we were careful not to make a sound. Three feet from the door, a man stepped into the doorway. Caught by surprise, I quickly noticed it was Gooch. He lifted his gun and fired as I heard Kendra gasp for air.

SNOOK

Sirens grew louder as I came closer to consciousness. Something weighed me down as I tried to move. My mind was fully aware, but my body moved in slow motion. I realized that I was holding Kendra's hand. As I came to I remembered what happened. I tried to lift myself up, which caused her body to slide to the floor. I saw blood splattered all over the egg shelled wall. Lying in a puddle of blood that we'd accumulated underneath our bodies, the excruciating pain from my head caused me to feel nauseous. I looked at my hand after grabbing my forehead and noticed it was covered in blood. I turned to Kendra and called her name with no response.

Police officers rushed through the front door yelling commands, but I couldn't figure out what they were saying. When help arrived, I could allow myself to relax and get help for Kendra. The paramedics tried to attend to me, but I insisted that they help her. One of them stayed with me and took my vitals. After learning I was shot in the shoulder and hand, I knew none of my injuries were life threatening. I was prepped for transport to the hospital as they continued to care for Kendra. They placed her on a stretcher and rushed her out of the house.

I was mad as hell as my adrenaline pumped. I couldn't believe that someone tried to kill us. Kendra didn't look good, and I feared the worst. Gooch was the hired gunman, but I needed to know who was behind the hit. I knew it was only a matter of time before the streets would be talking.

CHAPTER 43

Marlon

At home chilling, I watched the game and had a few beers to relax. Suga was out shopping for the baby nursery with a decorator she hired. My phone rang, and I noticed it was a number I didn't recognize. Leery, I answered in case it was a client.

"Yo. I'm in the hospital," Dee said frantically. "We were shot and Kendra may not make it."

"What?" I asked in disbelief.

"For real man, we were shot," Dee repeated now even more frantic.

Dee explained that Gooch showed up and left them for dead. Kendra's most serious injury was the bullet lodged in her head. Dee's injuries were not life threatening.

It was a happy time for Suga, and I hated that I had to call her with more bad news. Although she and Kendra were no longer friends, she needed to know what happened. I dialed her number and took a deep breath as I waited for her to answer.

"Hey, baby. I need you to come home right away," I said nervously.

"For what? You know I'm meeting with the decorator for our son's nursery. Let me tell you what I have so far—"

"I know baby, but I need to talk to you. Come home, it's important," I interrupted.

"What's wrong?" she asked.

"Something happened at Kendra's. Look, I want to talk to you face to face about this. You know how you get," I said cautiously.

"Stop treating me like a child Marlon and tell me what the hell is going on!"

"Dee and Kendra were shot last night, but Destiny was at her grandmother's house. They are both in the hospital. Dee will be okay, but Kendra isn't doing too well," I said. "I thought you would want to know. Do you want me to take you to the hospital?"

"For what? I don't want to see her. Did you forget that we aren't friends anymore? I have to go. Just let me know if anything changes. I will talk to you later," she said coldly.

"Are you sure you're going to be okay?" I had asked before I heard the dial tone.

Surprised by her response, I looked at the phone as though I was talking to a stranger. I knew she probably hated Kendra for what she'd done, but they did love each other at one time.

CHAPTER 44

Suga

I planned a dinner for my mother. There was unfinished business between us and since we hadn't spoken it was important that I made things comfortable. She'd moved out after our fight, which left a sour taste in my mouth. Moving out was best so that she didn't upset me even more. I was pregnant, and stress was the last thing I needed. An apology was needed, and our past could no longer be swept under the rug. I needed her in my corner.

I sent her a text message, which asked her to join me for dinner at my house. Her response led me to believe that she was more than happy to take me up on my offer. After a couple of hours, my mom showed up for dinner. As I hoped, she had her bags in hand.

"Girl, it smells good in here. If I didn't teach you anything else, I taught you how to burn on that stove," she said.

"I'm so glad you're here!" I wobbled to her.

I wrapped my arms around her and held her tight as I inhaled her scent.

"Baby, if you are inviting me then I'm here," she said, holding me tightly. She stepped back as she took a good look at my protruding belly. "Look at you. You're getting so big! You remind me of myself when I was pregnant with you, all belly," she said, turning me around slowly.

I smiled as I rubbed my belly with excitement.

"Come on, we have a lot of catching up to do," I said.

I grabbed her hand and led her into the kitchen.

"Where's Marlon? If you don't mind me asking," she asked hesitantly.

"He'll be home later. That gives us plenty of time to talk. I missed you so much," I said, patting her hand.

We sat at the table that I decorated beautifully. I prepared grilled chicken, vegetables and lit candles that created a calm mood.

"First, I want to apologize for being disrespectful to you. I know I shouldn't have spoken to you that way," I said, as I looked at her with compassion.

"I'm sorry for putting you—"

"I know and I forgive you," I said while interrupting her. "I understand why you feel the way you do. I apologize to you as well. I find myself in the same situation with Marlon. Now that I'm pregnant, I feel like I would do anything for him," I said. I rubbed my belly.

"What did he do now?"

"Oh no, calm down. It's the Kendra situation. I still can't believe he had sex with her. He wants to blame it on the alcohol, but he knew what he was doing. He was drunk with me before and trust me, he is fully aware of what he's doing. Kendra is in ICU, and her family may be taking her off of life support any day now. I know I should care, but I don't. I hate her for what she's done to me.

"Oh my, God! I'm so sorry to hear that. Have you seen her yet?" she asked.

"No! I don't plan on seeing her. I don't care what happens," I replied uncaringly.

"Now wait, she must've been a friend at some point. I know what she's done, but you can't sit here and tell me that you don't care about her."

"I'm not going to see her. To be honest, I wanted her to die! Why did she do that to me? I always knew she was jealous, but I never thought she'd go after Marlon."

"Suga, I think you should see her one last time. Once she is gone, you will never see her again. Trust me, you don't want her to leave this earth with that on your conscious," she said.

"I don't want to talk about her. I have something else I need to talk to you about before Marlon gets home," I said while peeking out of the window.

"Girl, you have more drama than a little bit. Let me take my blood pressure pill before you drop this on me," she said, reaching into her purse.

I took a deep breath as I thought about how I'd tell her.

"Please don't judge me, okay?" I said cautiously.

"I'm not God, but I will speak my mind. You have to know the difference."

"Well, Dee was the one that told me about Kendra and Marlon. He lied about Marlon being the father of Kendra's baby. He used that to get me to sleep with him," I said.

"Girl, I know you didn't! Now don't tell me this could be his baby," she said, throwing her hands in the air.

"I really don't know."

My mother's smile turned into a frown. She realized I wasn't joking.

"What do you mean you don't know? You better know that it's your husband's child. How could you do something stupid like that? Girl, if you know like I know, you will keep your mouth closed and live happily ever after."

"That's the plan, but I think Dee is going to be a problem. He knows that this baby could be his. He used me to get back at Marlon, and I let him. I don't know what I'm going to do. I know I shouldn't wish death on people, but I did. That's how serious this is. Right now Dee is in the way," I said.

"Now look, I know how far things can go in these situations. Don't ruin your life the way I did. You may not get a second chance and even then, your luck will run out. If I could take back what I did all those years ago, I would. It's too late for me. I loved a man so much that I killed my sister for him. Because of it, my sister is gone, and your father is behind bars. We all lost in that situation, and you've suffered the most. I don't want you following in my footsteps. You don't want to live this way."

"Then tell me what I'm supposed to do. Marlon is going to kill me if he finds out," I said desperately.

"Everything will be fine. Trust me, things have a way of working itself out when you least expect it," she said.

Kendra's condition had deteriorated. Her family called to ask me to go to the hospital to see her. I had given every excuse I could think of not to visit her. I didn't want to tell them the real reason I didn't want to see her. After pondering on the thought, I realized that it was my last chance to say goodbye.

When I arrived at the hospital, I was greeted by Kendra's family and Dee. In a weird way, I felt sorry for him. I'd never seen him like that. He was hurting, and it showed through the dark bags under his sleepless eyes. The family appeared to be defeated and helpless. Their sadness brought me to tears. I slowly entered Kendra's hospital room. It brought back the same feelings I'd felt when I thought about my mom after her death. It made my stomach hurt as I heard the machines beeping. I walked closer to the bed. It was dark in the room with only the lights from the noisy monitors. The smell of the hospital cleaning solution made me nauseous.

As I looked at Kendra, I didn't recognize her. Her tightly bandaged head was swollen, and her eyes were black and blue. It was apparent she'd lost a lot of weight. The tubes that pumped fluids and air into her body were strung about the bed. I watched the machine pump air into her lungs as her chest rose up and down.

"I'm so sorry this happened to you. I wish things could've been different between us," I said.

I held Kendra's cold, lifeless hand. With each breath she took, I was reminded of the good times that we shared together. Including the ones when Kendra held me up when the anxiety attacks took over. She was the reason I met Marlon, and she helped me to come out of my shell. In the end, she was the one there for me.

I put my arms around my friend for the last time and wept. I cried out from the pain that we'd caused one another. I tried and convicted her of the same crime that I too was guilty of. Before leaving, I kissed her on her swollen cheeks.

"I forgive you. I love you," I said.

A tear fell from Kendra's eyes. I wiped her tears and kissed her again. That was the last time I would see my friend.

It was the day before my baby shower and after a long night of lovemaking with Marlon I was exhausted. I joked that he would force me into labor if he'd kept stroking me the way he did. With the baby due any day, we wanted to have as much sex as possible. I enjoyed our little escapades, and I was as freaky as I was before getting pregnant. Marlon loved it. After collapsing from exhaustion, I was awakened by a sharp pain.

"What the hell is that?" Marlon said.

He rolled over into a wet spot on the bed.

"Oh my, God! My water broke!" I screamed. "We've got to get to the hospital!"

I didn't want to panic, but I was on the verge.

"Shit! What did you say?" he said, leaping from the bed with a wet T-shirt and boxers.

"My water broke. The baby is coming!" I repeated.

"Are you sure?" he asked nervously as he frantically searched for his pants and shoes.

"Yes, baby, make sure to grab my bag. I'm not in that much pain so calm down," I assured him.

Marlon extended his arm and helped me to my feet. Because of my size, I often needed help getting up from the bed and the couch.

"Come on, mama. You're beautiful even while in labor," he said jokingly.

Marlon tried calling my mother while packing the car. My bags were packed for the three of us. On the drive, he cautiously ran through each stop sign in the neighborhood as my labor progressed. The hospital was fifteen minutes from our home. With my contractions being more rapid, the drive appeared to be much longer. I breathed as instructed in one of my birthing classes.

"Did you get in touch with my mom?" I asked while breathing heavily.

"Who?" Marlon asked.

Not used to the fact that Sable was my mother, he looked at me strangely.

"Sable. Teesa. You know who I'm talking about!" I yelled in frustration.

"I didn't. Her phone kept going to her voicemail. I'll keep trying, baby. Just breathe," he said, as he held my hand.

SNOOK

Marlon's first born was finally ready to come into the world.

"I hope nothing has happened to my mom. I haven't spoken to her since yesterday."

Marlon remained focused on me, ignoring what I said regarding my mother. When we arrived at the hospital, he pulled up to the entrance of the emergency room. Frantically blowing the horn, a nurse ran outside with a wheelchair.

"Someone is coming," I said through my heavy breathing.

Once inside I was wheeled to labor and delivery while Marlon took care of my registration forms.

Several hours later, Marlon Dwayne Cole, Jr. was born. He weighed eight pounds, with ten fingers and ten toes. He was perfect. After ten hours of labor, he came into the world kicking and screaming. Exhausted from the delivery, I almost ended up with a cesarean with junior's big head. I didn't want a scar across my belly. I planned on bouncing back from this pregnancy and getting back into my two-piece bikini.

As expected Marlon's family and Uncle Redd were there offering their support. His parents were proud that Marlon finally had a son. They arrived with diapers, bibs, sleepers, and anything else needed during our hospital stay. Marlon and I were grateful that our loved ones wanted to share that special moment with us. I was filled with joy that my son was surrounded by love. I smiled at the thought of finally performing a selfless act by giving Marlon a son. I knew it was the best thing I could've done for him. He was proud to be a father and hadn't stopped smiling since little Marlon's arrival. He hardly let anyone else hold the baby for more than five minutes. A family was all he'd ever wanted.

CHAPTER 45

Marlon

*E*xcited about the birth of my baby boy, I couldn't take my eyes off of him. His eyes and nose were like mine, and I was glad his hair was good like his moms. I thought I'd give the family an opportunity to spend time with him, so I stepped out to get cold drinks for everyone. Heading back to the room, I noticed Dee in the hallway of Suga's room. He'd become distant since Kendra's funeral, so I was surprised to see him. I gave him the space he needed. As I approached him, it wasn't hard to notice that he'd lost weight. He appeared to be disheveled and different.

Either this man doesn't give a fuck or he's getting high, I thought. Either way he was fucked up.

"Hey, what's up man?" I asked, startling him when I spoke.

"What's up? Congratulations!" Dee said while smiling.

"Thanks, but how did you know? I didn't get around to making any phone calls. Things happened so fast," I said.

"It's cool. I stopped by the store to pick up my necklace, and they told me where you were. You did your thing as usual on the necklace. I wanted something for my baby girl in remembrance of Kendra, thanks, man," Dee said sadly.

I took a mental note to fire my new employee. No one tells a customer where I am. That was unacceptable.

"Well, can I see my godson?" Dee asked as he peeked around the corner into the room.

I led him to Suga's room where she and Uncle Redd were talking.

"Hey family, where's my godson?" Dee asked excitedly.

I noticed Suga pause as her eyes showed concern. She shifted in the bed when she saw Dee in the doorway. It appeared the blood drained from her face as her mood quickly changed.

"What's wrong? Are you all right?" Uncle Redd asked.

"Nothing, I suddenly feel sick. I have a headache," Suga responded dryly.

Smiling, Dee reached over to see the baby. Suga quickly pulled back as she held Marlon Jr. close to her.

"Let me see him. What's wrong?" Dee asked sarcastically.

"No. He's sleeping right now. The nurse is on her way to take him back," she said, frantically looking for the nurse's call button.

I paid close attention to Suga and Dee's interaction. The sudden change in her mood was strange.

"I came up here to see my godson and you're about to send him back to the nursery?" Dee asked.

Leaning again to see the baby, Suga wrapped him tightly in his blanket. "No! I said he's asleep," she said coldly. "I'm tired, and my baby has been passed around enough," she said.

"Come on man. Now is not a good time. I'll walk downstairs with you," I said, looking at Suga strangely.

"Oh, I forgot," Dee stopped in his tracks. "I brought something for the little man."

Dee turned back and handed Suga the gift bag. Pulling out two outfits, a pair of sneakers, and a sleeper, he proudly placed them on the bed. He made sure to place the bib in front of me that read, *I love my daddy.* Suga grabbed the gifts and quickly stuffed them back inside of the bag.

"Yeah, he looks like me," Dee said sarcastically. "No, I'm just fucking with you, Suga. Relax," he said while laughing.

I noticed him give Suga a wink as he walked out of the door. I wanted to kill his ass. Pissed off at his sly comment, I knew I had to confront him.

"What in the hell was that? You should know better than to fuck with my family," I said. I stood nose to nose with him.

"Yo, I said I was joking! You and Suga are all uptight and shit. I was trying to make her laugh," Dee said.

"That shit wasn't funny, it was disrespectful!"

"What's up with you? Stop tripping."

"What the fuck were you trying to say in there, man?"

"I don't know what you're talking about, but you need to chill," Dee said, as he backed away. "I told you I was just fucking with her stuck up ass. What the fuck are you implying?" Dee asked.

At that point, Uncle Redd came out into the hall. Standing between us, Dee and I continued to stare each other down.

SNOOK

Uncle Redd held his hands on our chests to keep us apart.

"The two of you need to handle whatever this is about another time. This is a hospital, not the streets. Marlon, Suga needs you in there. Dee, it was nice seeing you again, but it's time for you to go," Uncle Redd said.

"I apologize to you both," Dee said.

"That shit rubbed me the wrong way. Don't hurt yourself with your jokes," I said. I walked back into the room.

Mad as hell, I was sure Uncle Redd noticed the fire shooting out of my ears. I knew exactly what his implications were. I had to know what Suga had to say about the situation. She faced the window as I walked up to her. I fought the urge to flip her out of the hospital bed. After the bathroom incident, I knew she could no longer be trusted. Somehow, I convinced myself that I was the only man she'd been with.

She was in tears. She wiped her face with the back of her hand. I grabbed her shoulder, turning her toward me.

"Suga, what in the hell is going on here? Why are you crying?" I asked.

"I'm happy. We have a beautiful baby boy now—"

"I don't want to hear any more of your lies," I said interrupting her. "You had a nigga fooled all this time! First, you're fucking bitches, and now you're fucking my boys, too?"

"I'm not fucking anyone but you! How could you accuse me of something like that? I'm your wife!"

"Wife?"

"Are you crazy or something? I would never do something like that to you, especially not with him," she said. She pointed towards the doorway.

I bent down and kissed her deeply. Thinking she'd won the argument and avoided a train wreck, I moved my hand up to her neck and held her by her throat. Choking her with one hand, I unzipped my pants. Suga scratched at my hand as she tried to get it from around her neck. I needed her conscious for my next act of rage.

She gasped for air while reaching for the nurse's call button. I yanked the cord as it fell to the floor. She tried to leap for the phone as I knocked it down to the floor.

"Marlon, please—" she said while gasping for air.

"Is he my son?"

"You know he's yours. Don't do this, Marlon, please," she pleaded.

Uncle Redd came back into the room after hearing the commotion. I quickly zipped my pants back up. I let her go and stood in front of her.

"Is everything okay in here?" he asked.

Still fuming, Suga forced a smile on her face.

"Yes, it's fine. We have some things to talk about; that's all. Why don't you go home, you've been here all day," Suga said.

"I'm going to ask again, is everything okay, Suga?" Uncle Redd repeated, ignoring Suga's request. "Maybe you need to take a walk son."

"You heard her," I said.

"Suga if you need me, call me. Marlon, that's my baby, and before you think about doing anything stupid, maybe you should leave and calm down. If you do something now that you'll regret later just remember there is no coming back," he warned.

SNOOK

"Uncle Redd, it's okay. Go ahead so that we can finish talking," Suga said.

"Baby, are you sure? I don't have anything to do today. If you need me, I'm here," Uncle Redd reassured her.

"It's fine," she said.

As soon as the door closed behind him, Suga leaped off the bed. Trying to take cover in the bathroom, I blocked her. I carried her back to the bed without saying a word. I dropped her on the bed as she kicked and tried to scream. I covered her mouth keeping her cries for help from escaping.

"If you scream I'll kill you. I promise," I whispered into her ear.

I slowly removed my hands from her mouth as the fear in her eyes was evident.

"Marlon, please don't hurt me. I didn't do anything, I swear! Baby, I love you. Think about your son—"

"My son?" I interrupted. "You better hope like hell he's mine. I want a blood test!" I said. I looked at her angrily.

"Let's not forget what you did with my best friend. Don't act like you're innocent," Suga said.

She fought back.

"Yeah bitch, you're a hoe. I treated you like a queen when I should've treated you like the rest of them hoes. As a matter of fact, suck my dick bitch! You want to be a hoe than I'll treat you like one," I said. I unzipped my pants.

"Hell, no! You suck your own dick. You're not going to talk to me like that and expect me to suck your dick!" she said, as she fought to get away.

"If you bite me, I will choke the shit out of you," I said.

I prepared for the best head ever.

Trying to stand up, I pushed her back down on the bed as I pulled out my erect dick. I stroked it as Suga looked like she wanted to scream to the high heavens. Forcing my penis into her mouth, she gagged from my violent plunges.

"You like it, don't you bitch?" I asked as I violently moved in and out of her mouth.

After several minutes, I released all of my anger into her mouth. I looked at her in disgust as I slipped back into my pants. I left out of the room without saying a word.

CHAPTER 46

Suga

S obbing and disgusted by Marlon's acts of rage, I lay in the bed and stared at the ceiling while wishing I was dead. I needed my mother, and she was nowhere to be found. There was no way in hell I would have a paternity test done. I was sure that Dee was the father of Marlon, Jr. I noticed his strong characteristics that I couldn't ignore. I wanted to kill myself, but realized that would leave my son alone. I decided to come up with a plan if my life depended on it.

I asked God to forgive me of my sins. There was so much to confess, but He already knew that. I needed to mend my broken marriage. I needed God to show favor to my child by allowing Marlon to be the father. That seemed to be the answer to my problems. I'd be able to move on with my life, but I knew that would be too easy.

The nurse came to check on me and greeted me with a warm smile. She could tell that I was upset.

"I'm going to take your vitals now, ok? Your blood pressure is slightly elevated," the nurse said. I lay in silence as she continued to write in my chart. "I can give you something to help you sleep if you want. Sometimes new moms go through something called post-partum depression. Make sure to speak with your doctor about it," she added.

She rubbed my back, trying to comfort me.

"Okay, I will speak with her about that. Can I see my son?" I asked while wiping my tears.

"Of course. Do you want me to bring him to you? Or do you want to go to the nursery?" she asked.

"I'll go to the nursery," I said, as I got up from the bed and slid my feet into my slippers.

She'd advised that she would return with my medication. I walked down to the nursery to see Marlon Jr. I arrived in time for his feeding and was able to feed, rock, and put him to sleep. I loved and missed him just for the brief time we were apart. Holding him close and kissing him over and over, I was determined more than ever to be the best mother I could be.

When I returned to my room, there was a rose and a card on my bed. After reading the card, I realized they were from Marlon. I tossed them in the trash and climbed back into bed. The nurse entered the room, informing me that Marlon had left shortly before I returned. I gave her a phony smile as I took my pills. I lay back while waiting for the pills to take effect. My mind raced with plans on how I would get away

SNOOK

from Marlon. Rest was what I needed because the next day was planning day. I finally gave in to the drowsiness and drifted off to sleep.

CHAPTER 47

Marlon

I returned to the house still enraged with anger. The answer to my question could be waiting at home on my personal computer that was password protected. I'd designed a special wedding ring for Suga. A microchip was placed in her ring all those years ago. The logger that was installed was used to track her movement every hour, which provided entries twenty-four hours a day.

One of my clients owned a security company and provided me with the technology needed to keep tabs on Suga. Every month I took her ring to be cleaned, but I downloaded data and performed general maintenance on the G.P.S. The data was stored on a server, which I could access from my personal computer.

When I gave her the ring, I tracked her every move for the first six months. It was hard to believe that she was all mines. I looked hard, but never found anything suspicious.

SNOOK

I'd call her just to see if she'd lie about her whereabouts. She never did. After a while, I accepted that she was one of the good ones.

When I stopped tracking her was when the trouble began. If I had continued a little while longer, I would've known what she was up to.

I sat at my computer, regretting the mistakes I made. I tried to rationalize Suga's actions. I slept with a lot of women. I was wrong, but the karma that came back on me was far more than I could handle.

CHAPTER 48

Suga

The sun shined brightly through the hospital window. I pulled the covers over my head as I tried to forget the things that have happened in my life. I could feel a presence in the room. Fearing it was Marlon, I quickly turned over to see who was there.

"Suga, it's only me," my mother said. "How are you feeling?" she asked.

She hugged me, wearing her usual shades and hat.

I held her tight as I thought about how I never wanted to let her go.

"Where have you been? We were worried about you," I said.

"I know you were. I've been laying low. Somebody figured out who I was, and that's not good for any of us right now. I didn't want to bring my drama to your home, so I stayed away. You can understand that can't you?" she asked.

"Yes, but who knows about you?" I asked curiously.

"I ran into Trey at your store, but I can't say for sure that he recognized me. I just couldn't take the chance," she explained.

"How would he know it was you?" I asked.

"Trey worked for your father. He treated him like a son. He trusted Trey. I heard that he was the one that helped take your father down. He started following and harassing me about your father's money after he was locked up," she said.

"Where is all this money he supposed to have stashed somewhere? I haven't seen one red cent of it," I said curiously.

"Look, enough about me. How is motherhood? Where is my grandbaby?" she asked, looking around the room.

"He's in the nursery. I'll have the nurse bring him to the room. As for motherhood, I haven't had time to take it all in with all of the drama," I said, as I reflected back on the last few days. "Dee came to visit, acting as if he was the father. Marlon damn near lost his mind. Now he wants a blood test and you know I can't do that. I'm just not sure if he's the father or not. I don't want to lose my family over this, but I don't know what to do about it," I explained.

"That damn, Gooch! If he had been on his job that night, this would've never happened!"

"What do you mean?" I asked as I looked at my mother strangely.

A feeling came over me as she moved around suspiciously.

"Nothing… Just know that your mother would lay her life on the line for you. I have nothing else to lose. My life is over Suga, and all I can do is try to make my wrongs right. All this is my fault," she said sincerely.

I believed every word. I was floored at another one of my mother's confessions. There was nothing I could do about it now.

"I don't know what to say. I just don't know—" I responded hesitantly.

I was beginning to fear her. I didn't know her anymore, and life caused her to no longer be the gentle, soft-spoken person I remembered. Mentally, she was someone else.

"You continue to pretend that you don't know, okay? Now, where is my grandson?" she asked as she took a deep breath.

When the nurse finally brought Marlon Jr. into the room, he came with peace and contentment. My problems were far away, and he became the most important thing in my life. My mother picked him up and held him close to her. I watched as tears flowed from her eyes.

"Oh Suga, he's so beautiful," she said. She rubbed her nose against his face.

"I know he looks just like me doesn't he?" I asked proudly.

"Child please, I bet you wished he looked like Marlon right now," she said jokingly.

We laughed, but privately I wished he did. There was a knock at the door that startled us. She handed the baby back to me and gathered her things. She walked into the bathroom. She hoped to come earlier to avoid running into anyone.

"Good morning," Marlon said with a big smile.

"Good morning," I said puzzled as I watched my mom come out of the bathroom.

Watching him closely, I didn't expect Marlon to be in a good mood. He walked over and kissed Marlon Jr. He leaned in to kiss me. Pulling back slightly, I accepted him with apprehension. I looked over at my mother.

"Somebody is in a good mood this morning," she said sarcastically.

"Why not? I have everything a man could ask for. I have a beautiful wife, a new son, and money. Man, I can't wait to get them home," he said excitedly.

"Well let me get out of here. I'll see you tomorrow, right?" she asked.

"Yes, we're supposed to go home tomorrow," I replied.

She kissed Marlon Jr. and left out of the room. Marlon and I sat in silence. Not knowing what to say, I passed Marlon Jr. to him so that I could go to the bathroom to freshen up. My hopes were that he'd get a chance to bond with him and forget about wanting a paternity test. When I returned, Marlon was changing the baby's diaper.

"You're changing his diaper all by yourself?"

"Yes, I've seen it done before. It wasn't too bad," he said as he smiled proudly.

I returned the gesture with the hopes that maybe we would get past all of the drama we'd been dealing with. Marlon laid the baby down and took me into his arms. It felt right as always, and that's why I ultimately fell in love with him.

"I'm sorry about yesterday. I was so angry at the shit Dee pulled. I still need to know the truth," Marlon said, as he kissed me on my head. "Even if the truth hurts, I need to know. You slept with Dee didn't you?" he asked.

"No, I didn't! Why do you think I slept with Dee? Whatever is going on between the two of you is your problem, not mine. You have expectations that I have no way of living up to. I'm human, and I have and will make mistakes, but fucking your boy is not me. Let's not forget the fact that you slept with my best friend," I said defensively.

"I always thought that snake wanted you. Then he comes in here pulling that bullshit. I swear to you if I find out you fucked him I will kill the both of you," Marlon threatened.

"If you didn't sleep with Kendra then maybe you wouldn't be so suspicious," I said.

"Okay, you're right, and I was wrong, but damn it Suga! You got me thinking some crazy shit right now!"

"You're thinking crazy shit? What the hell do you think I'm thinking after the way you treated me yesterday?" I asked. "I don't know how we've gotten to this point. We've both fucked up! Either we're going to work it out or we're not, but our son will not suffer from our mistakes. I love him more than I love myself."

"So, are you saying that he is mine?" Marlon asked.

"I've never said anything different. I love you Marlon, but our relationship is going to scary levels. How could you treat me that way? I'm your wife and the mother of your child," I cried.

"You've shown me that from your past behavior. First, in the bathroom at the club and now this. I don't know who the fuck you are. You had me tricked all this time, but I see who you really are. You've been behaving strangely, but I haven't said anything," Marlon explained.

SNOOK

"Marlon, just leave it alone! Trust me when I tell you it's not what you're thinking. Let it go or leave me the fuck alone! I'm done with this. Get out!"

I realized that there was no way that Marlon would let it go. The accusations were too much for me. It was finally clear that only a paternity test would clear his mind.

"I can't do this anymore, Suga," Marlon said, leaving the room.

"Neither can I," I replied.

I allowed myself to shed a tear. I was proud of myself for finally standing up to him.

When Marlon opened the door, there was a commotion out in the hallway. The shouting and scurrying caused me to get up from my bed. What was happening in the hallway drowned out the drama that was unfolding inside of my room.

CHAPTER 49

Redd

O n my way to Suga's room, I heard someone call my name. When I turned around, I noticed Sable, but the familiar voice addressed me the way Teesa would've. Startled, she took off running as she noticed the strange look I'd given her.

"Teesa, is that you?" I called out. Running to catch up to her, I had to look into her eyes.

"Teesa stop! I just want to talk to you!" I yelled out.

When I approached her, I grabbed her by the arm. She fought to break my grip, but I held on tightly. As she screamed, she attracted attention from the nurses, patients, and visitors.

"This game you're playing is up. What in the hell is going on?" I asked with tears in my eyes.

"Let go of my arm! You're making a scene that I don't need," she said.

Afraid the police officer on duty would be called, I let her go. I watched as she dropped to the floor in tears. It appeared the years of running and pretending had finally caught up to her.

"How did you know?" she asked.

"I didn't until now, but it had crossed my mind a few times. Teesa, you and Sable were twins, but there were distinct differences between the two of you. You have your walk and Sable had hers. You had a slight limp from when you broke your ankle when you were ten years old," I explained. I knelt down beside her, as I looked her in the face. "How could you abandon your daughter? You fucked her life up, and she's still paying for your sins."

"I know and I'm sorry for it all. If I could take it all back, I would. I'm trying to make things right. Sable was a bitch, and you know it. She slept with Suga's father behind my back and didn't give a damn how I felt. I hated her for that," she cried.

We stood to our feet as she slipped off her glasses and looked me in the eyes.

"Does Suga know?" I asked.

"Yes, I told her a while back. We've been working on our relationship and one day I hope she'd find it in her heart to forgive me. I hope you'll do the same," she said, as she laid her head on my shoulder.

"You don't need my forgiveness. You need to forgive yourself."

The nurse's station alarmed security of the actions that were taking place on the floor. When security approached us, Teesa panicked and took off running towards the stairs. I yelled for her as one of the security officers ran after her, while the other officer questioned me. She almost made it to the door, but she was grabbed by the officer. I watched as she kicked, scratched, and punched the officer as she tried to break free of his grip. I explained to the officer that everything was all right, but it was too late. Suddenly, Suga approached us in the hallway.

"Mom! Let her go!" Suga screamed.

Suga charged towards the officers, but I held her back. She continued to cry out for Teesa. I was sure she feared that it could be the last time she'd see her. Suga collapsed in my arms.

CHAPTER 50

Teesa

I was a nervous wreck after being stopped by the officer. I knew that my presence was too much for everyone. Suga collapsed in the hallway when she saw the officer restraining me. She'd been unconscious for three hours, and I didn't want to be the cause of Suga not getting well. She was a mother and needed to be healthy for Marlon Jr.

"Doctor, she's awake!" I yelled when Suga opened her eyes. "Thank God you're alright. You need to stop scaring me like this," I said. I rubbed the top of her head.

The doctors rushed over to her and checked her vitals. The doctor requested that the family keep her calm and relaxed during her stay.

"Where is Marlon?" Suga asked.

Uncle Redd and I looked at one another. Not wanting to upset her, we avoided the question.

"How are you feeling? You scared us to death, girl. The doctors want to keep you here for a couple more days for observation," I informed her.

"I thought they were going to lock you up—"

"No, everything is fine," Redd interrupted. "I talked to them and they let her go. I told them that we'd just had a little family dispute."

"Oh, so you know? Uncle Redd I didn't want to keep that from you," Suga said to Redd

"Don't worry about that. This is between me and your mother."

"I'm glad that Marlon isn't here. I need to talk to both of you. Marlon and I aren't going to be together. I'm not going back to that house. He can have it all. I just want to be free of him. I have money saved and need to get on my feet. I want to stay with you, Uncle Redd. At least until I find a place for me and the baby," Suga explained.

"You know that you're more than welcome to stay with us. Are you running away from him or is this a decision that you've both made?" Redd asked.

"We both agree that this is what's best. He is questioning the paternity of our child. He has every reason to, but I plan to make sure that it doesn't happen," Suga said.

"I support you and any decisions you make," I said.

"How do you plan to keep him from having a paternity test? Do you think he's going to let you keep him away from his son?" Redd asked.

"No, that's why I plan to stay with you until I can get my own place. He's not coming anywhere near him. If he isn't his child, I don't know what he'll do. I have to protect my son," Suga said.

I filled Redd in on the situation with Marlon and Suga so that someone else was aware of what was going on. I didn't know how much longer I could run around Richmond before my luck ran out. First, Trey and now Redd. I hated the thought of leaving Suga and my grandson, but I had to make a move and quick.

I knew that there were many things I should've said to Suga, but instead I let her vent while I devised a plan that I knew wouldn't fail. There was no way that she could keep Marlon from his son. He had resources, money, and lawyers at his fingertips. She didn't think rationally and was guided by fear.

CHAPTER 51

Redd

I looked the place over one last time. My project was completed years earlier but needed some finishing touches. I'd put the old photos away in a box and placed them in the closet. There couldn't be any reminders of the past. The new paint, fixtures, and furniture could never hide the tragic ending of one's life. Admiring the work that I'd put into the place, it was finally ready for Suga and the baby. I didn't know if she'd accept her inheritance or run away from it. One thing was for sure I wouldn't know until I tried. Sadness crept in as I remembered Sable and Teesa sitting at the table in a heated game of spades. Sable always competed with Teesa. I shook my head thinking that I never knew that the competition would have led to Sable's demise.

SNOOK

I headed to the hospital to pick up Suga and the baby as planned. I wanted her and the baby safe from Marlon's rage. In a way, I felt guilty for some of the decisions that she made, but I also held Teesa responsible. She needed companionship and a way out, and Marlon seemed to be the man to offer it to her. Besides, I knew he truly loved her.

Most of the time I was right, but I'd forgotten to factor in Suga and her intentions with Marlon. He had the means to take care of her.

All hail to Redd for creating this monster, I thought.

When I arrived at the hospital, I noticed Marlon walking across the parking lot. I was relieved that Suga and the baby weren't with him. I noticed he was reading a piece of paper as he rushed to his car. I hurried inside not knowing if I was too late or if Suga had decided to run. As soon as the elevator stopped, I rushed down the hall towards her room. I found her and the baby safe. I took a deep breath as I watched the nurse going over some paperwork with her. I damn near had an asthma attack trying to get to her.

"What's wrong?" Suga asked, as she noticed my disheveled appearance.

"Nothing, I thought I was late. Go ahead and finish up, while I take the bags to the car," I said.

"Did you bring the car seat?" Suga asked.

"Yes and it was safely installed by the fire department as you requested," I said.

I wanted to make her laugh as I noticed the concern on her face.

"Thank you."

She continued listening to the nurse's instructions as I walked back to the car.

I pulled up to the front door as Suga and Marlon Jr. were wheeled out to the car. I helped put the baby in his seat as the nurse made sure that I buckled him in properly. Suga was still sore from the delivery. She shifted in her seat to find a comfortable position. She waved to the nurses as we drove off.

CHAPTER 52

Suga

I became nervous as I thought about the responsibility of being a mother. There would not be any nurses or doctors to assist with late night feedings, diaper changes, or anything else. I glanced out of the window as random thoughts ran through my head.

What if I lose him? No, how could that happen? What if I forget about him one day and leave him? No, that would never happen. What if—"

I quickly cleared my mind of any negative thoughts regarding my ability to parent. I knew we were safe at Uncle Redd's house. I enjoyed living with him when I was younger, but there's nothing like having your own.

I sat in the back seat watching Marlon Jr. as he slept peacefully. I looked at how tiny he was in comparison to the car seat. Uncle Redd drove carefully on the busy highway.

"You passed the exit," I said with confusion.

"Just ride. I know where I'm going," Uncle Redd replied while peeking at me through the rearview mirror.

"I hope you're not trying to take me back home. I told you, I'm never going back there."

"Just ride," Uncle Redd ordered.

He drove another twenty minutes into the city. I grew more anxious as I wondered where we were going. After several minutes, it was clear where he was taking us. I remembered the tree-lined streets and neatly manicured lawns. He turned onto the street where my mother and I used to live.

"Why are we on this street? This is where I used to live," I said nervously.

We pulled into the garage that I remembered playing with my friends. We'd pretend that we owned the vehicles parked in the garage.

"I don't understand why you're bringing me here. I don't want to be here. There is nothing here for me but lies and bad memories."

"I know that you don't want to be here, but I need you to hear me out. Just come inside before you say anything else," Uncle Redd instructed.

I looked at him like he'd lost his damn mind. As much as I wanted to curse him out and demand that we leave, I allowed him to prove his point. Knowing there may have been a good reason that he'd brought us there, it didn't prevent the pain that he was stirring up inside of me. Although my mother was alive and well, my aunt died in that house and finding her dead body was traumatizing.

I looked around the neighborhood, which hadn't changed

much. The property owners kept up the neighborhood, and I smiled when I saw two little girls riding their bikes down the sidewalk. I'd ride my bike back and forth down the same sidewalk until the street lights came on. I took a deep breath as we approached the freshly painted house. The exterior was updated with natural colors giving the house a grand appearance. I remembered it being dark and drab when I was younger.

Uncle Redd opened the door as butterflies filled my stomach. I felt like a scared five-year-old on the first day of school. I wanted to cover my eyes with my hands and peek through my fingers. When I looked inside, I expected everything to look the way it did when I was a child. I imagined myself kneeling down beside my mother's dead body. Reality quickly sat in as I remembered that Sable's body was the one I'd held in my arms. Once I cleared my mind of the painful memories, I looked around the house.

The house was immaculate. The walls were now gone, which gave way to an open floor plan that showed off the high vaulted ceilings. Everything was new from the paint, furniture and shined hardwood floors.

"Oh my God! This isn't anything like I remembered. I love it. It's like a brand new house," I said, admiring the décor.

"Don't get too excited. The renovation is not complete. When your father found out that I was having the place renovated he demanded that the upstairs not be touched. He doesn't even want anyone up there," Uncle Redd explained.

"I wonder why?" I asked. I thought back to the letter and

the mysterious key my father had given me. "I didn't know she still had this place," I said, as I walked around, looking at the beautifully shined floors.

"She doesn't. This was your father's place, and now it's yours. I was the overseer of the renovation down here. I thought you might want to sell it, and that's why I renovated it. It's up to you. I rushed out and bought new furniture for the place and voila," he said while smiling.

"Thank you so much! I love you, Uncle Redd," I said, giving him hugs and kisses.

"It's paid for. Here is the paperwork that should be signed, but it's all yours," he said. He handed me the paperwork.

I guess that's the least Linwood could've done for me, I thought.

"You did all of this for me?" I asked.

"It took some time of course, but yes I did. I knew you would come back here one day, but not under these circumstances. The most important thing was to make this place like new. I didn't want you to relive that day," he said. He put his head down.

"I must say you've done a fabulous job."

"You and the baby should be safe here. Give yourself some cooling off time, and then work things out with your husband when you're ready. Remember, you can't run from your problems," he said.

"I know. I just need time to think. He has done things to me that I just don't think I can forgive him for," I replied sadly.

"Everything will work itself out. I stocked the fridge. Your mother will be by with the baby's things. You feel comfortable staying here alone?" he asked.

SNOOK

I watched as he walked around checking the windows.

"Oh yeah. I'll admit I was leery when we arrived, but I'm sure we'll be fine. As you said, you can't run from your problems," I said.

"I better get going. The upstairs is the same as it was. Your father demanded that no changes be made until further notice. After all these years, he hasn't given me any other notice. Make sure to be careful if you go up there," he advised. Uncle Redd gave me a hug and walked towards the door. "Hey Suga, make sure to lock the door behind me," he said while closing the door.

CHAPTER 53

Redd

Pulling out of the garage, a horn blared. As I looked out of the rearview mirror, I noticed it was Trey. He was the last person I'd expect to see in the neighborhood.

"What's up? What are you doing around these parts?" Trey asked.

He was driving a black tinted Range Rover. From what I could tell, he was alone in the truck.

"I was just getting my niece settled in. You?" I asked curiously.

"I have a friend that I visit from time to time, you feel me?"

"I feel you."

"Are you talking about Suga?" he asked.

"No, my other niece," I said. I tried to draw attention away from Suga.

SNOOK

Since Trey's name came up during Linwood's investigation, I decided against telling him that it was Suga.

"Well, I have to get going," I said, as I rolled up my window and sped off.

Discomfort rode next to me. I thought that I'd made a mistake by leaving Suga and the baby alone. No one but Teesa knew where she was, and that was one too many. Against my better judgment, I decided to head home and check on them later. I prayed that I didn't deliver her to the devil.

Suga

I sat the car seat on the sofa as Marlon Jr. slept. Getting settled in would be a slow process. I began by unpacking our bags and putting the baby's formula in the refrigerator. What Marlon and I went through was still unsettling. I didn't decide how I would handle things with him. While going through my handbag, a business card fell to the floor. I suddenly realized it was the card from the detective who'd investigated L.C.'s murder. I picked up the card and stared at it, contemplating if I should place the call that would keep Marlon away for a long time. I picked up my cell phone and slowly dialed the mobile number. I counted to five and pressed the send button. The voicemail immediately came on.

"This is Suga. I have some information on the murder of Linda Cunningham. I think my husband Marlon may have had something to do with it. You were right, we were lovers, and he found out about it. I'm not sure, but he could've been involved," I said nervously.

As I hung up, I couldn't believe what I'd done. I placed my hands over my mouth to hold in my outcry. I cried silently knowing that I may have sealed his fate. Convincing myself that it could be the only way to hide my secrets, I knew that protecting myself was first and foremost.

Marlon, Jr. began to fuss, so I fed him and put him back to sleep. I glanced at the string that hung from the attic staircase. Curiosity killed me as I remembered that Uncle Redd said that my father wanted it to be left untouched. I ventured up the stairs to face the demons that had been left. When I got to the top of the stairs, I remembered seeing my father make several trips up the secret staircase. As a little girl, I tried jumping up and down to reach the string, but he'd never allowed me to go into the attic with him.

I pulled the string and let down the ladder. Dust fell, causing me to cough and sneeze. Looking up to see a door with a padlock, the silver key I'd recently began wearing around my neck fit perfectly. I opened the lock and pushed the heavy metal door open. The ladder creaked under my weight as I tiptoed up the stairs.

The dark attic was warm. I tugged at the silver chain to turn on the light above my head. Although it was clean, the air was thick and filled with mildew. I looked around for the attic window. Air would be good for the stuffy room. I noticed the old dollhouse that my father had gotten me for Christmas when I was eight years old. It was in the corner covered with dust. I walked over and tested the doors and windows to see if they still moved properly. I walked to the window and opened it halfway to let in some air.

I stumbled over two tall boxes while surveying the area. They looked strange and out of place. Pulling back the flaps on one of them, I found a box of sheets and blankets that smelled of musk. I closed the box, opened the other box, and found stacks of papers and books that didn't interest me. Before I closed the box, I saw the back of a picture frame. I picked up the gold frame and turned it over to find my baby picture. I smiled as I was reminded of the family I loved. A tear fell as I thought about how life changed for me and where I was presently. I tucked the picture under my arm so that I could take it with me. There were two plastic tubs that were pushed far into the corner of the attic. As I opened the first tub, it was filled with jewelry and other valuables.

Who do these things belong to? I thought.

As I opened the second tub, the smell of cash smacked me in the face. There were stacks of money secured with rubber bands and neatly stacked. The recognizable scent let me know it was real. Like always, the scent stimulated my center.

"Yes! Thank you, Jesus! Oh my God!" I screamed out.

This was my sure way of having a fresh start.

"Thank you, daddy!" I yelled. I dragged the tub down the attic ladder.

I danced down the stairs as the tub dragged behind me. As I pulled the tub across the shiny fresh hardwood floors, suddenly things were looking up. I also brought down the tub that was filled with the valuables. I placed them both in the closet.

After several minutes, I heard a knock on the door. With

the baby in tow, I remembered Uncle Redd had informed me that my mother was bringing the baby's things. When I opened the door to my surprise, I was greeted with a pistol in my face. As I stared at the gun, fear came over me like a tidal wave.

"You scream, and I'll shoot," Trey said, as he looked at me angrily.

Forcing his way into the house, he grabbed a chair and pushed me down into it. I watched helplessly as he taped my legs and one arm behind my back. Placing Marlon Jr. in my free arm, I tried to remain calm as he frantically prepared to do harm to us.

"Where is it?" he shouted.

"I don't know what you're talking about," I cried.

"The money Linwood stashed," he said, as he began flipping over the cushions on the couch.

"What money?" I asked.

"Bitch, if you keep lying to me, I'm gone blow your pretty little brains out all over your baby. You got that? Now think before you speak. Where would he stash his shit? I've been looking for years. When I saw that bitch Teesa, I knew she'd lead me to it. Your mom did my boy dirty so here we are," Trey said furiously.

"Please don't hurt my baby. He has nothing to do with this," I pleaded.

I held him tightly with the one arm using my lap to support his body.

"Teesa, now that's a gangster bitch. She left my boy to rot. That gold digging bitch was back for something, and I want it," he said, as he waved the gun around in anger.

"I don't know what you're talking about. I swear. I just left the hospital with my son. I haven't been here since I was a kid."

"The night your father was arrested he was weighted down, but none of the money was recovered. If Teesa had the money she'd already be gone, so that leaves you, baby girl," he said as he cocked his pistol.

"You can search the place. Just let us go, please," I begged.

I struggled to hold the baby with my one free arm. He placed the baby back in the car seat, and I became hysterical from being separated from him. I watched as he continued to flip over furniture and pull out drawers. The more he searched, the angrier he became. As he walked to the closet, I became nervous as I hoped he didn't find where I had hidden it. I tried thinking of a way to distract him from finding it.

"Why are you doing this to me? There isn't anything here. Can't you see that this place has been renovated? If there was anything here, it's gone. My mother probably spent all of his money a long time ago," I tried to convince him.

"Shut the fuck up! If you're not telling a nigga where the shit is, shut the fuck up!" he yelled.

"Fuck you! Get the fuck out of my house! Help! Somebody, please help me!" I screamed as I tried pulling out of the tape my legs were bound with.

Trey ran over and hit me with the butt of the gun, knocking me to the floor. As blood oozed out of the gash on my head, I continued screaming. My vision was impaired. He placed a piece of tape across my mouth. Marlon, Jr. fussed, which distracted him from putting a bullet in my head. Dazed and disoriented, my bearings were compromised. I felt myself slipping into darkness as the sound of Marlon, Jr.'s cries faded away.

CHAPTER 55

Teesa

&xcited about spending time with Suga and the baby,
I hadn't taken the time to think about the idea of
going back to the house. I figured no one would
think we'd go back to where it all began.

I managed to use the key and open the door. With my
arms filled with groceries, the baby's bags, and Suga's luggage,
I managed to make my way to the door. I was able to get
some of Suga's things while Marlon wasn't home.

"Hey, Suga! Come help me with these bags, please!"

As I entered the house, I was thrown to the floor. I could
see Marlon Jr. in the car seat crying. A few feet away, Suga
lay bleeding from her head and unconscious. It took three
seconds for me to realize the danger we were in. Realizing it
was Trey, it was clear he was there for what he thought

SNOOK

Linwood left behind. While on the floor, my survival mode immediately kicked in. I reached into my bag and grabbed my gun.

"Get the fuck up, bitch! Where the fuck is the money?" Trey yelled.

"Ok, please don't shoot," I pleaded.

As I rose to my knees with my back facing him, I whipped around quickly and fired my gun at him.

CHAPTER 56

Marlon

A lot happened, and I hoped Suga and I could return to normal. She opened her eyes three weeks and three days after the shooting. She was in the intensive care unit with Redd and I by her side. I had a paternity test done. Thankfully, the results came back proving that Marlon, Jr. was, in fact, my son. It killed me not knowing for sure if he was. The situation between us had gone too far and had to be resolved. The past was now done, and neither of us could take it back. I promised the future would begin with our son. I prayed that Suga would forgive me for treating her horribly. I too would find it in my heart to forgive her.

I was awakened by the loud beeping noises from the machines. I saw Suga frantically trying to get up from the bed.

"Doctor! Doctor!" I called out. I tried to calm her down.

SNOOK

She reached for the tubes that had provided her oxygen for the last few weeks through her nose. Uncle Redd grabbed her hands as the doctor and nurses rushed to her aid. Once she'd calmed down, the doctor calmly explained where she was and why. Her hip was shattered by a bullet, she had several broken bones, and the gash in her head required several stitches.

She moved around and mumbled, "My baby?"

"Our son is at my parent's house and he's fine. Try not to worry about him and get well. We need you, baby," I said sadly.

With a confused look on her face, her eyes asked many questions.

"I had a paternity test done at the hospital before you left. I couldn't wait for you to come home because it was killing me. I kick myself every day for what happened to you. If I weren't such a jerk, you wouldn't have been there in the first place. I'm hoping to put all of this behind us and move on with our lives. I only want you to get better so we can be a family again. I'm so sorry, Suga. I love you. Please, forgive me," I cried, as I laid my head down on her.

"Yes," she mumbled, as tears rolled down her cheeks.

"I'm sorry for everything. I promise I will be a better man for you, and the best father I can be for our son."

She mumbled, "Mom."

"She didn't make it, Suga. I'm so sorry, baby. She saved both of your lives," Uncle Redd told her.

I thought about how she'd thought she lost her mother once, but this time she wouldn't return. Suga cried hysterically as we tried to console her. We knew the right thing to do was to let her grieve.

Suga endured weeks of physical therapy. A rod was placed in her hip during surgery, which required grueling physical therapy sessions during her hospital stay. The therapy was painful, but the idea of playing in the park with Marlon Jr. in a wheelchair was all the courage she needed. Fighting to pull through her deep depressions, visits from Marlon Jr. helped her to regain her strength.

I prepared the house for her return. In hopes of putting the pieces back together, she was ready to get back to her duties of being a mother and a wife. Although she'd completed her physical therapy, she couldn't take too many steps without the use of a walker or cane. On the way home, she asked me to stop by her father's house. Thinking it wasn't a good idea, I hoped to talk her out of it.

CHAPTER 57

Suga

I had to return to the house to retrieve my money. The way things had changed, I had no choice but to return home with Marlon. I believed that was where I belonged, in my house with my child. I couldn't wait to get back to all of my belongings. I didn't have to do much for him to take me back.

"I'm not taking you back there. We're going home so you can forget it," he ordered.

"I have to go back. I left something that was very important. If you don't take me, then I'll go on my own."

"No. There's nothing there for you. It never was," he said.

"It will only take a minute. I promise I will never go back there again," I said persistently.

"Ok, but let's make it quick," he said.

As we pulled up to the house, we sat in the car in silence. I looked at the house with the yellow police tape still dangling from the front door. That was where all of my problems began and ended.

I opened my car door as Marlon quickly jumped out to assist me. I reached in the back seat for my cane. My resilience would not allow me to use my cane. I placed it back. Still sore, doing things on my own was something I had to learn.

"I'm okay. I can do it," I said in a frustrated tone.

"I'm going in with you," he said.

"No, I have to do this myself. Trey is dead. He can't hurt me anymore. Please let me do this on my own," I said demandingly.

"Are you sure you want to go in there alone?" he asked.

"Yes, please wait here," I said, slowly walking up to the door.

With Marlon waiting outside, I returned dragging a taped plastic tub. Marlon rushed over as he looked at the tub strangely. I placed old photos of my family on top of the tub, which allowed him to assume that the tub was filled with family heirlooms. I went back in and returned with another tub. Marlon lifted the heavy tubs into the trunk.

"What's in here?" Marlon asked.

"Some things I wanted to keep," I said with a smile.

I looked back at the house for the last time. The *For Sale* sign in the front yard overpowered the size of the house that at one time appeared to be so big. The cleaning crew was scheduled to be there in a week to get the house ready for the open house. I was thankful for a new beginning in life. I wasn't sure what the future had in store for me, but I was ready. A new Suga had awakened after the tragedy. I was no longer weak and easily manipulated. I had a greater purpose in life and Teesa's survival instincts gave me the courage to live through anything. Linwood was a leader and businessman, which taught me to have business smarts at all times. It was in my blood to survive by any means necessary.

"It's going to feel good to be back at home," I said.

I took a deep breath after realizing that it would be my first time home as a mother. Marlon hesitated before pulling out of the driveway. He turned towards me and looked at me caringly.

"Promise me that you'll never leave me like that again. I don't care what we're going through," Marlon pleaded.

"I promise," I lied. "Where's my baby? Is your mom going to bring him over?" I asked.

I unbuckled my seat belt and took my time getting out of the car. My hip ached from the ride and gave me some resistance while trying to stand. Marlon extended his arm to hand me my cane, which I again refused.

"He is in the house waiting for you. My mother has been helping out while you were in the hospital," he said.

"That's why I love her. I'm so glad that we have her to help. I'm sure I'll need it," I said.

"You know you're going to have to use this cane, right?"

"I'm not using that cane. It makes me look like an old woman."

I held on to Marlon's arm and limped into the house. As much as I wanted to pretend that we would be a happy family, I knew that would be reaching too far. Being under his thumb, I'd no longer be controlled by his insecurities. I was determined to be my own woman. I loved my new found freedom and wanted to live life to the fullest. I had to let go of all my fears. I loved him, but I was no longer in love with him. I was determined to make him pay for what he'd done.

"Surprise!" family and friends shouted as we walked through the front door.

"Wow! Thank you," I said tearfully.

I was completely taken by surprise. The house was decorated with welcome-home banners, balloons, and streamers. Marlon's mother brought Marlon Jr. to me. Seeing I wasn't able to stand any longer to hold my son, Uncle Redd pulled up a chair for me to sit down on.

I held him for the first time in our home. It felt good to be a mother. Marlon Jr. grew fast. I kissed him and told him how much I loved him. The feeling of happiness overwhelmed me. I was greeted by our guests one-by-one as they hugged and kissed me. For once, I didn't feel nervous or anxious about my future.

"Suga, I'm glad to see you're feeling better. Still looking good I see," Dee said slyly.

"Thank you, Dee," I said with a forced smiled.

I reached for him and whispered into his ear, "In case you didn't know, he isn't yours so don't try that shit you pulled at the hospital again."

"I know and I'm happy for you," he whispered back.

We broke our embrace as the heat rose between us. There was no denying there was still sexual tension between us. I hated the feeling but knew I had to ignore it before I'd end up in the same situation. I didn't want Marlon to accuse us of sleeping together, and Dee was still a dangerous situation.

SNOOK

"Hey man, are you enjoying the party?" Marlon asked Dee, as he kissed me and Marlon Jr. proudly.

"Yeah man, this is nice. You know if you need anything just let me know," Dee said.

"I appreciate it, man. You know I never had the chance to apologize about what happened at the hospital," Marlon said.

"Don't worry about it. You know I have a sick sense of humor sometimes," Dee said.

"Well, guys excuse me. I'm going to take the baby upstairs," I said through the loud music.

I reached for my cane as Marlon and I laughed. I hit him on the leg with the cane as embarrassment showed on my face.

"Are you sure you don't need help?" Marlon asked.

"No, I can do it. Thanks, baby. I want some time alone with my son," I said. I slowly headed up the stairs.

The nursery was just the way I wanted it. My mom had done a great job making sure the nursery was complete. I placed the baby in his crib as I sat in the glider and admired the beautiful decorations. I missed my mother's presence and knew I'd never forget her. Again, there was no closure except that I knew she was really gone this time.

At least she was able to see her grandson, I thought to myself.

"Hey you," a voice called from the doorway.

"What in the hell are you doing in here?" I said with a slight whisper.

Dee stood in the doorway, stroking his penis through his pants.

"Marlon wanted me to let you know he was making a beer run," Dee said with a smirk on his face.

He stepped into the nursery as I jumped up and stopped him from coming any closer.

"Get out of here. What are you doing?" I asked nervously.

Dee took my hand and slid it down into his pants. His erection craved me and fought its way out.

"Hell no! That shit is over. I don't want you, and I never did. Now get the fuck out of my way!" I said, pushing past him.

He grabbed my arm and pulled me close to him while pressing his penis against my stomach.

"Oh, so you're going to take it?" I asked, looking him in his eyes.

"No, you're going to give it to me," he said, as he rubbed his hands up and down my back.

My center throbbed at his demand. The risk excited me.

He has some balls thinking he's going to fuck me right here in a house full of people, I thought.

"Get the fuck out of here, Dee! If you don't, I will scream. Now let me go!" I yelled.

One more run? No, I couldn't do that, I thought.

"He won't be back for at least twenty minutes. Come on, you know you want it," he said while kissing and groping my breast.

My heart pounded in my chest as I quietly moaned. My mind told me *no,* but my body screamed *hell yes.*

"No, I can't do this," I said, yanking my arm from his grip.

"Suga, I need you. I need you bad," he said passionately.

He pulled out his penis, hoping that I wouldn't be able to resist it.

"Put that back! Are you trying to get us killed! Dee, you have to go," I said, as I pointed to the door.

SNOOK

Dee had a pretty penis and fucked me just right. Marlon was good in bed, but Dee was better and rougher. I wouldn't have minded one for the road, but the stakes were much higher. I walked towards my bedroom with part of me wanting to fuck him where he stood, but the other part of me wanted him to leave and never return. Dee caught up to me and pulled me into the hall bathroom. He gently picked me up and placed me on the sink. He covered my mouth with his lips while choking me with his long tongue. He dropped his pants and pulled down mine. Before I knew it, he was inside of me.

"No! Dee, stop," I moaned quietly.

"You want me to stop?" he asked, moaning in my ear.

He was sexually excited, and he pounded me harder and faster.

"Please! Stop you're hurting me!"

I mustered the strength to push him off of me and grabbed my pants off the floor. I rushed to my bedroom and locked the door behind me.

"Fuck!" I said while cleaning myself.

I couldn't believe what had just happened.

I looked into the mirror at myself, realizing that this would never end.

"No more stupid ass mistakes," I said, as I put water on my face.

I pulled my hair back into a ponytail revealing the scar that extended from my scalp to my temple.

"Damn," I mumbled. I traced the scar with my finger. It was a constant reminder of my brush with death. I dabbed some concealer on the scar. Although it was barely visible, I knew it was there. I took a deep breath as I forced myself to look at my reflection in the mirror. I felt much stronger than before, but I saw the sadness in my eyes. I returned to the party as if nothing happened.

"Hey, girl!" Santé screamed when she saw me.

She ran towards me with open arms.

"Santé, is that you?" I asked. I smiled at her with excitement.

"Yes, it's your favorite cousin!" she said.

"Last I'd heard you were in New York," I said.

I was happy to see my cousin. My father's sister lived in New York, and they visited in the summer. We were the only children in our families, and we were equally spoiled. We lost contact after I moved in with Uncle Redd.

"It's still like looking in the mirror," Santé said.

"But I'm much cuter," we replied at the same time while laughing.

"I missed you so much," I said.

"Well, I'm here for a few weeks. That should give us plenty of time to catch up," she said.

"I have something to talk to you about before you leave," I told her.

"Sure, but I'm not going anywhere. All you can eat and drink, that's what I will be doing," she said.

I was able to enjoy the rest of my night despite the run in with Dee. I had too much at stake to allow him to be a distraction. I had a plan that had to be executed flawlessly. That was if I was to maintain what was rightfully mine. There was also some unfinished business that I didn't know how to rectify. I made a huge mistake by reporting Marlon to the police, and I had to figure out a way to get him out of it without giving myself away. There was business to be handled and the right person for the job was in place. Money was definitely on my mind.

"Meet me out in my garage in five minutes," I whispered to Santé.

She nodded and continued playing her hand in spades. I went out to the garage where I'd hid the two containers. I placed the one filled with cash on the top shelf of the garage and stacked old newspapers on top of it.

"Remember when we used to pinky promise that we wouldn't tell each other's secret?" I asked, holding out my pinky finger.

"Of course I do," Santé responded, grabbing my pinky with hers.

"I have something to show you. I'm going to need your help getting rid of this," I said, as I lifted the lid off of the tub.

"Damn! Where did you get this stuff?" Santé asked.

She knelt down as she examined the contents.

"It doesn't matter. I know you have connections in New York. Do you think you can pull it off?" I asked.

"Of course I can. This is what I do, remember?"

"Thick as thieves, right?"

"For life," Santé responded.

"Be careful. I don't want you going back to prison for this. I would feel bad if that happened after asking you to do this for me."

"I run with the boss now. I won't be anywhere near the

deal when it goes down. Let me make some calls and get things in line. From what I can tell, you're looking at a big payday, girl," Santé said.

"No, we're looking at a big payday," I said, hugging and giving her a high five.

I closed the lid and slid the tub back under the shelf. I walked Santé to the back of the house where she was parked. Marlon led the last of our guest to their cars. My plan was to get rid of the valuables at the highest price that I could. The money would be placed in my rainy day fund. I knew it would rain like hell because it had never failed to before. I deserved the things that happened to me, but I'd be ready for the next downpour.

"Baby, where have you been?" Marlon asked.

"I was outside talking to Santé. Thanks for everything, babe. I love you so much," I told him.

"I love you to death, Suga," he reminded me.

I pulled back and stared at him. Uneasiness crept between us and forced us apart.

"That's not the kind of love I want Marlon. I need you to love me for me. I have my issues, and I know I'm not perfect. I want to be comfortable in my own skin. I'm not proud of my past, but it's all a part of who I am. I'm not the same person you married. I'm so sorry for hurting you," I said boldly.

"This is the first time you've ever told me what you wanted," Marlon said.

"You have controlled our business and this marriage. I need a voice in this marriage. Don't get me wrong, I appreciate everything we have, but what do I have?" I asked.

SNOOK

"Suga, you have everything. I work hard to provide for us. What more do you need?"

"I don't have access to some of our accounts. The only money I have is the money that you give me when I ask. That's not right! I work just as hard as you do, and I deserve to have my own money."

"Where's all of this coming from? You never complained before."

"No, I didn't complain. I didn't know any better, and I let you control me. I'm your wife, not your child," I said, as I paced back and forth with frustration.

"I know who the hell you are. Let's talk about this later."

I could tell he was angry by the tone of his voice. I watched as the vein in his neck pulsated. I decided to walk away, but the conversation wasn't over. I wished I'd done this a long time ago.

CHAPTER 58

Marlon

My phone call was interrupted by one of the staff who informed me that two detectives had arrived to speak with me. When I came to the front of the store, I noticed it was the same detectives that came over regarding L.C.'s murder.

"Marlon Cole, I have a few questions for you. Why don't you come down to the station with me so we can get this matter cleared up," Detective Wilkes said, as he browsed the jewelry case.

"And what might this little matter be about?" I asked.

I stood tall as the detective attempted to intimidate me.

"We can talk privately if you'd like," Detective Wilkes said.

I led the detectives back to my office. I led them to the seats that separated me and Suga's desk. I closed the door and sat on the corner of my desk.

"Did you know your wife's friend Linda Cunningham?" Detective Moore asked.

"No, I didn't. Why?" I asked.

"We have reason to believe that your wife may have murdered Linda Cunningham and is setting you up for the murder," Detective Moore said.

"What? Suga wouldn't do something like that. I don't know where you're getting your information, but you're wrong," I said in a frustrating tone.

I walked around to my chair to sit down. The thought of Suga accusing me of murder was difficult to believe. I just wanted Suga to think that I had something to do with it. I was an innocent man. All I wanted was for L.C. to leave town and never show her face in Richmond again. She was supposed to take the money and leave.

"When we came to your home that morning, we weren't sure if Suga was our suspect. We discovered some disturbing voicemails left by your wife on Linda Cunningham's cell phone during the days leading up to the murder. Your wife called stating that she had reason to believe you had something to do with the murder," he advised.

"Suga isn't the person you're making her out to be. She didn't kill anyone, and she didn't sell me out," I said.

Detective Wilkes reached into his pocket and pulled out a phone. He placed the phone on my desk as Suga's voice came through the speakers.

So, you don't want me after you fucked up my marriage? That shit you pulled at the club was foul! Now I need you, and you think you're going to turn your back on me? You love that bitch more than you love me? I can't believe you chose that bitch over me! I will kill you and that bitch! You won't get away with this shit. You're dead bitch, believe that! Suga screamed as the message ended.

Now with chills running up and down my spine, the next message was Suga saying exactly what the detective said. She tried to rat me out to the police.

"What the fuck is this?" I asked.

I grabbed my head in disbelief. I couldn't believe she would do this to me.

"I'm sorry, but this is a disturbed woman. We've been trying to build a case against her but have been unsuccessful. You were our last resort. Is there any information that you can give us that might help our case?" Detective Moore asked.

I still wasn't sure if Suga had anything to do with the murder. I'd never trusted the police, and I wouldn't start then and I wasn't about to start.

"No. This is the best you can do? You come in here and accuse my wife of murder because you want a confession from me. Well, detectives, I'm sorry, but you've wasted your time," I said, regaining my composure.

"All right, then it could be your funeral next," Detective Moore said, standing to his feet. "This is a dangerous woman who needs help," he added.

"I have a business to run gentlemen," I said, standing to my feet as I led them to the door.

As soon as they left, I called Suga at the house. There was no answer on the house phone. I called her cell phone, and surprisingly there was no answer. I rushed out of the door and headed home.

SNOOK

Suga's car was in the driveway. I rushed through the front door calling her name.

"Suga! Where are you?" I yelled. I went from room to room looking for her and the baby. They were gone.

I went into the kitchen where I found a letter on the refrigerator held by a magnet.

Marlon my love,

If you're reading this, I'm already gone. I'm sorry for the things that I've done, but I can't change the past. Life has a way of making you pay for your sins. I don't know how I found myself in my mother's shoes, but I am. Love our son more than you love yourself. Tell him every day how much I love him. I left him with your mother. If I knew then, what I know now, Karma could kiss my ass.

Love,
Suga

AMARQUIS PUBLICATIONS
PRESENTS

KARMA'S KISS 2
COMING SOON